JEN

A BORDER COLLIE'S TALE

– An Old Farm Dog Reflects On Her Life –

peter kerr

Oasis-WERP

Published by Oasis-WERP 2021

ISBN: 978-1-5272-9838-5

Copyright © Peter Kerr 2021

www.peter-kerr.co.uk

Cover design © Glen Kerr

Typeset by Glen Kerr

ABOUT THE AUTHOR

Best-selling Scottish author Peter Kerr is a former jazz
musician, record producer and farmer. His award-winning
Snowball Oranges series of humorous travelogues was inspired
by his family's adventures while running a small orange
farm on the Spanish island of Mallorca during the 1980s.
Peter's books, written with warmth, gutsy style and spiky
humour, are sold worldwide and have been translated into
several languages. He is married, with two grown-up sons,
and lives in East Lothian.

www.peter-kerr.co.uk

TABLE OF CONTENTS

– ONE –

EAST LOTHIAN, SCOTLAND – 1983

'JUST YOU LIE there beside the car, Jen … like a good dog.'

I've seen the day, not so long ago it seems, that I'd only have lain here 'like a good dog' until the Boss was out of sight. But these days … well, I'm getting on a bit now – about fourteen in human years, they say – and the sunshine's fine and warm, so I won't bother tiptoeing after him to see what he's up to this morning. Anyhow, I don't suppose he'll be doing anything I haven't seen before, and many, many times at that. Castrating calves, most likely. A batch of them arrived last week, complete with nuts, I noticed, so they'll be for the snip today, I reckon.

That'll be why he's got that vet chap with him. It's his car I'm lying beside in the yard here, incidentally. I've always thought vets' cars smell funny – not in a humorous way, you understand – but more sort of strange. Well, strange for me at any rate. All disinfectant and chemical-like. Medicines and worm mixtures, stuff like that. You see, being a collie, and a Border collie at that, I'm what you might call a 'nature girl', and it's the smells of *natural* things that appeal to me. Things like the smell of newly turned soil when I'm following the Boss's tractor at ploughing time. Things like the tangy whiff of the midden when he's loading the dung-spreader on a frosty day. Things like the smell of sun-warmed straw at harvest. Even the nostril-nipping hum of the hen house when it's getting a much-needed muck-out by the Boss's wife. Aye, things like that. *Natural* things. Oh, and of course, I like the way I smell myself: fur all nice and imbued with aromas of the farm, which are too many and complex to describe, and with subtleties I'm afraid the human nose is incapable of appreciating. I learned that sorry fact a long, long time ago…

'THAT DOG STINKS to high heaven!' declared the Boss's wife, about a couple of months after I took up residence on this wee spread. 'She's mingin'! Just look at those dangleberries clinging to her rear end!'

'Ach, they're just sticky willies,' the Boss shrugged. 'Just weed seeds – nothing to bother about.'

'No, they are *not* just sticky willies, and don't you even *think* of allowing her into the house again when my back's turned!'

The Boss just smiled that wee smile of his. 'Yes, yes, whatever you say, dear. Whatever you say.' Then he gave me a wink, and I knew right away we were still on the same wavelength.

You see, that's the thing about humans who understand dogs: *they* know that *we* know what they're thinking. Trouble is, *they* have to use words to communicate, whereas we dogs don't. That's why we have to laugh when we hear them saying: 'Oh yes, a *very* clever dog, that. Understands every word you say, you know.' Well, even the dumbest human should realise that's about as relevant as saying a dog would be good at painting the barn door, or making a five-bar gate, or playing the bloody bagpipes, for God's sake! When attempting to communicate with humans, we always try to get across to them that the thoughts are ours, while the words are purely theirs. Unfortunately, it isn't a concept many humans are capable of grasping.

But I digress. In case I forget (and I'm the first to admit that I *am* getting a wee bit forgetful at times), I'd better explain the background to that comment the Boss's wife made about me being 'mingin'. Oh, and another thing, if you're getting the impression that there's a bit of friction between the Boss's wife and me, I can assure you that nothing could be further from the truth, even though my calling her the 'Lady Bitch' may suggest there's a hint of animosity on my part. The opposite is the case, and I'll tell you why.

It's simple. Firstly, I regard her as a lady, and no less a lady than I regard myself. Also, she's a female of *her* species, and the term 'bitch' is the one used to define that gender in canine circles: the one that comes naturally to *me*. So, in every respect, my referring to the Boss's wife as the 'Lady Bitch' is no more a slight against her than it would be if the title were applied to me. Which I readily do – and I hold no-one in more esteem than I do myself. It follows, then, that a state of mutual respect should exist between us. And it does. It's just that we have our own standards, our distinct sets of values and, not surprisingly, they differ in certain aspects.

I don't deny she's pretty, though. Not, of course, with the same kind of *animal* beauty I've been blessed with myself. I mean, you wouldn't expect anyone to say of the Boss's wife that she has lovely markings – lustrous black hair all over her body, with a white bib and matching socks, a nice shiny nose, and sharp-eyed as a fox. Nor would you hear anyone say to the Boss when seeing his missus for the first time: 'Bonnie-lookin' wee bitch ye've got there, pal. She'd throw fine pups, ye ken. Aye, get her served while she's young. She'll have a fine big litter in her, and ye'll make yersel' a right pile o' money for nothin'.' No, you wouldn't expect that to be said of her. But all the same, I must admit she *is* bonnie enough, in her own way. If only she wouldn't pollute herself with all that man-made scent stuff. Sickly-smelling flowery stuff. Not that I've anything against flowers, I should stress. Certainly not. But once again, I come down on the side of the more robust *natural* variety: dandelion, sow thistle, hogweed, even the wild garlic you find growing in the woods around here. Nothing better than a roll in the latter to keep the flies off in summer, by the way.

And this brings us back to the matter of the Lady Bitch calling me 'mingin'', which, for those of you unfamiliar with the Scottish vernacular, can mean anything from a bit 'whiffy' to downright breathtakingly repulsive. An element of 'unkempt' is often implied as well. Yet, while I confess to being somewhat miffed at finding myself on the receiving end of such an inappropriate expression, I don't hold it against the Lady Bitch. Indeed, I can understand her reasons. Almost. For the sake of harmonious relations, however, I prefer to treat her remark as merely an example of her own *particular* set of values, though regrettably misplaced in this case.

But more of that later. First, let me tell you how it all began...

*

OLD DODDIE RUNS a flock of sheep on a remote place up in the Lammermuir Hills, about ten miles south of here. He's a good shepherd, old Doddie: nothing he doesn't know about sheep, and a highly-regarded breeder and trainer of sheepdogs as well. All Border collies, naturally. And if there's nothing Doddie has to learn about sheep, the same can be said about his knowledge of collies. He isn't slow to point this out to anyone who shows the slightest interest, and even to those who show absolutely no interest at all.

'See them pups there,' he'd be known to say when showing off a new litter, '– well, Ah can tell at a glance the ones that'll make good workers, even if they're still no seein' right an' can hardly walk yet. It's a matter o' experience, ye see. A lifetime spent in the company o' sheep and collies. Yes, Ah was born tae it, just like ma father afore me an' his father afore him an' his father afore him, as far back as ye like tae go, like. It's in the blood, ye ken. Oh aye, Ah've a bloodline as pure an' unadulterated as a pedigree Cheviot ram. Nah, nah, there's none o' yer hybrid vigour in me!'

This was pretty much the spiel I overheard him giving the Lady Bitch the day she came to ask about buying one of his pups. That'd be about thirteen years ago now.

'Do ye, eh – do ye keep sheep yer*sel*', mistress?' he asked her coyly.

'No, we don't have sheep. Cattle, but no sheep.'

'Ah well, they're no bred for workin' cattle, these pups, so maybe ye'd be better –'

'No, no,' the Lady Bitch cut in, 'we're not really bothered about that. It's just a dog to have about the place we need. One to keep an eye on things, you know.'

Old Doddie's face lit up. 'Ye mean a kind o' watchdog – a yard dog, as the Yanks ca' them on the telly?'

'Yes, more or less. And, you never know, we can maybe get it used to working with the cattle in time. But honestly, that's not too important at the moment.'

Old Doddie stroked his chin, thinking. Opportunity was knocking when least expected, so the door would have to be opened smartish. 'Aha, so it's *that* kind o' dog ye're after, eh? Well now, Ah just maybe have exactly what ye're lookin' for.' Doddie was willing his hands not to start rubbing themselves together. 'If, eh – if ye care tae come wi' me tae this wee pen at the side o' the lambin' shed here, mistress, Ah'll – eh – Ah'll let ye see what Ah mean, like.'

And that was the first time I set eyes on the Lady

Bitch. Actually, it was the first time I'd set eyes on *any* female of the human species. Old Doddie had never bothered to take a wife himself, you see. 'Never saw the point,' he used to say. 'Bloody expensive articles tae keep, them – what wi' their falderal frocks an' vacuum cleaners an' fancy cookin' an' everything. Cream cakes an' four-ply toilet rolls – money-squanderin' extravaganceries like that.'

I was pleasantly surprised, therefore, to see how attractive this female human was. That said, any human, female or otherwise, would have appeared attractive compared to old Doddie, who admitted being the nearest thing to a living scarecrow you'd ever see – and proud of it.

'But,' the Lady Bitch protested when she looked into the pen, 'these aren't puppies, they're fully grown dogs.'

'Aye, three o' ma best students – next generation o' champion sheepdogs, like. Just a bit past a year old, an' shapin' up tae be grand workers.' Old Doddie cleared his throat. 'Well, eh, no countin' Jen, the wee bitch there, that's tae say. Mind you,' he hastened to add, 'she's a grand wee collie in every other way. She's just no got the knack o' workin' sheep like her two brothers there. Oh, and afore ye say it, Ah know ye'll be wonderin' how ma eagle eye for judgin' a pup failed me on this occasion. Well, let's just say Jen has a mind o' her own. Aye, she's a free spirit, ye might say, an' Ah've never came across another dug like her in ma entire puff.' Doddie had warmed to his theme to such an extent that steam was almost belching from his ears. He grasped the Lady Bitch's arm and whispered in tones of strictest confidence, 'Honest, hen, Ah couldnae learn her nothin'!'

Struck with the sudden realisation that he may have been a tad *too* candid in his revelations, Doddie then waited with bated breath for the Lady Bitch's reaction. 'Oh, an' just in case ye're worried aboot her nature,' he put in with some urgency, 'Ah can assure ye, mistress, that Jen has the canniest dispossession ye'll ever find in a collie. Very biddable in every way, just like her mother an' father an' many o' them afore her … except for followin' orders wi' the sheep, like. Aye, but clean in her habits, though. Never answers the call o' nature in among the sheds an' pens here – always away oot o' sight somewhere. Never shits in her own nest, so tae speak.'

Even as a callow youngster, I could tell that if Doddie didn't shut his mouth soon he'd blow his chances of getting me off his hands *and* trousering a tidy earner into the bargain. This bothered me, as I'd taken an instant liking to this human female. I liked her smile and admired the knowing way she looked at me. She understood. So, without wasting a second, I set about selling myself. Ignoring my brothers, who were diving about the pen like idiots, barking and showing off to their master, I sat quietly with my ears pricked, looking bright-eyed, alert and friendly, and most crucially, bombarding the Lady Bitch with we-were-meant-for-each-other thought waves. After all, being adopted by her could well be the best chance I'd ever get of finding a future away from old Doddie, who had made it abundantly clear that I had no future with him anyway.

It was simply that he couldn't accept what *he* judged to be my lack of discipline, in comparison with my brothers, for example. They took being trained to work sheep very seriously and were keen as mustard to please old Doddie in every way. And they *were* damned good at the job. I'll give them that. Anyhow, the difference between them and me was essentially that they regarded herding sheep as their destiny, a prerequisite of life as unquestionable as breathing. They enjoyed it too, whereas I saw working to orders as a chore. I preferred to do things my own way, to have some fun with the sheep during my training sessions. And I'd be telling a lie if I denied deriving some mischievous pleasure from turning a deaf ear to Doddie's frantic whistling and his roars of '*Come by*!', '*Away tae me*!', '*That'll do*!' and, inevitably, '*Lie doon*! *Lie DOON, ye hoor*!' By this time, the sheep would have scattered in all directions over the face of the hill, and I'd be lying there in the heather, delighting in their response to this unexpected taste of freedom. Freedom! That was what life was all about, wasn't it?

While it goes without saying that I knew what all those commands of Doddie's meant, it just struck me as a bit demeaning for an intelligent creature to be expected to obey them without question. And I admit in all modesty that I *am* an intelligent creature – more intelligent than old Doddie himself, if you want to know the truth. I mean, to illustrate my point, take one of his own favourite sayings: 'Tae be able tae train a dog, ye have tae let it know first an' foremost

that ye've got more between the lugs than it has.'
Then he goes and confesses to the Lady Bitch that he
'couldnae learn me nothin'!' I rest my case.

Of course, such a self-critical notion would never
enter Doddie's mind. And as it happens, I've found
over the years that this is a fairly common failing in
some humans: they're so stupid they think themselves
clever. And even sheep aren't as thick as that.

A perfect example was old Doddie's reaction when
he caught me playing 'Tig' round the dung midden
with a couple of orphan lambs one afternoon. This
pair of wee woollies had been bottle-fed since birth,
so were as tame as can be, and, just like me, were
always up for some fun as well. That's another thing
about most humans: they seem unable to get their
heads round the fact that so-called 'dumb animals',
given a chance and the right conditions, will get
along just fine with most other creatures. And this
goes for commonly assumed 'adversaries' like sheep
and sheepdogs as well. It isn't surprising, then, that
nothing could have been farther from old Doddie's
thoughts when he came round the corner that day and
caught me cavorting with the two orphan lambs –
especially since *they* were chasing *me*!

'What the fuck's goin' on here?' he bellowed, his
face crimson. 'Ah've always knew there was somethin'
weird aboot you, Jen – somethin' no just right. But
what the hell would any o' ma herdin' cronies say
if they saw *this*? A Border collie bein' rounded up
by two pet lambs, for Christ's sake! Honest, ye're as
thick in the heid as shite in a bottle, and ye'll be offa
this place the minute Ah find somebody daft enough

tae take ye away!'

And it just so happened that the Lady Bitch turned out to be that somebody. However, if old Doddie had entertained any hopes of her being 'daft', he was in for a disappointment...

'*How* much?' she piped.

'Just – eh – just the round hundred-and-fifty. Aye, a right bargain, considerin' her pedigree an' that. Best bloodline o' workin' collies this side o' Australia!'

'But that's just the point. She *is*n't a working collie. She's a free spirit, as you put it, and your price doesn't match your description.'

Old Doddie rolled his shoulders and surveyed his feet. 'Aye, well, that's as may be, mistress, but ye have tae appreciate Ah'm asking a fraction o' the price Ah would be askin' if she was fully –'

'Fifty quid! Cash! Take it or leave it!'

Old Doddie glanced up and cocked a heedful eyebrow. 'Fifty, ye say? Cash?'

'In crisp fivers. Bought as seen. No pedigree required.'

'Done!' The good shepherd grabbed her hand and pumped it heartily. 'But do me a favour, will ye?'

'A favour?'

'Aye, dinnae go breedin' wi' her. One Jen in the entire collie world is enough for any o' us tae be goin' on wi'!'

* * * * *

– TWO –

I THREW UP on the way home. I'd never been in a car before, you see, and I didn't respond to the experience very well at all. I didn't expect the Lady Bitch to take too kindly to the result either: a gooey dollop of semi-digested Wilson's Dog Meal deposited on the floor of her otherwise spotless Ford Cortina. But she just smiled (a somewhat strained smile, admittedly), patted my head and told me not to worry: no harm had been done. Then she opened the side window, stuck her head out and threw up herself. Kindred spirits, I thought. We'd get on famously.

I'd been watching her as she drove, and it was clear we had much in common. She had poise, style. It may not have been the same kind of poise and style I automatically displayed when herding sheep – or, more accurately, when *purporting* to herd sheep – but the similarities were there nonetheless. Even the way she puked through the car window had a graceful quality to it, a quality I had never known in my only previous experience of a human. For instance, I'd taken for granted that all humans would share old

Doddie's habit of smoking a pipe and spitting out of the corner of his mouth every few seconds. He also farted regularly – usually when spitting. I noticed the Lady Bitch did none of these things. Yes, like me, she had class, and we'd get along just fine.

What had disagreed with me on the journey was the bumping and swaying and shaking of the car as it bowled along. The thrumming noise of the engine bothered me too, as did the faint but inescapable whiff of petrol fumes. Those fumes would have been irritating enough on their own, but mixed with the Lady Bitch's fake-floral perfume, they were more than my super-sensitive nasal sensors could endure.

I had started the trip up-front on the passenger's seat, right where the Lady Bitch had indicated I should sit. And I found the views from this elevated position intriguing: an enlightening experience compared to what had been little better than a worm's eye view of my surroundings when creeping stealthily round huddles of old Doddie's sheep on some bleak hillside. But the novelty of seeing broad new landscapes whizzing past in a blur of colour soon conspired with those other alien sensations to make me feel dizzy, then slightly queasy. I decided to slip down onto the floor of the car, where I curled up with my face close to the Lady Bitch's left foot. But now the vibrations and thrumming noises seemed more exaggerated than ever, and the Lady Bitch's habit of pumping her foot up and down on a pedal thing didn't help either. I could tell a vomit was imminent.

Although I was no stranger to throwing up (it's a dog *thing*, particularly during aftermaths of competing 'at the trough' with a bunch of ravenous siblings), I had always done it in places where no human was around to take offence. In any event, the only human likely to be around would have been old Doddie, and he would have taken no more notice of one of his dogs puking in the bracken than he would a hen taking a dump on his window sill. But this in-car experience was different. I was acutely aware of that, and was pricked by a barb of remorse for having soiled the Lady Bitch's immaculate rubber car mat – not to mention her left shoe. But, cometh the problem for a collie, cometh the solution, and I promptly set about cleaning up the evidence of my 'mishap' in the way we dogs instinctively do. Which was when the Lady Bitch threw up for the second time.

That journey served as a lesson harshly learned for me, though, and I vowed there and then that no car would ever be graced with my presence again. Not if *I* could help it anyway.

*

'WELL, JEN, HERE we are at your new home,' said the Lady Bitch when we drew into the yard at Cuddy Neuk. 'And I don't suppose you're sorry the trip from your old one is finally over, hmm?' She patted my head again, then added under her breath, 'And you can take it from me you're not the only one!'

But she was all smiles as she opened the car door and ushered me out. My first impressions were good. Very good. This was a neat and tidy yard, the opposite of old Doddie's ramshackle scattering of tumbledown sheds and rickety sheep pens. Sure, there was a dung midden somewhere close by here as well – I could smell that plainly enough – but it was a nice, welcoming smell and I immediately felt at home.

The Lady Bitch was quick to notice. 'I see your tail's wagging, so that's a good sign.' She bent down and tickled me behind the ear. 'Yes, I'm sure you're going to like it here. And it's all yours to look after on your own. No other dogs to compete with.' She paused and looked at me with a lopsided little smile. 'Not, I suspect, that you'd give a hoot if there were.'

How right she was. This was my patch now, and woe betide any dog, cat, hen, heifer, pigeon, postman, bullock, salesman, crow or truck driver that didn't respect the fact.

'Anyway,' the Lady Bitch went on, 'have a good sniff around. I'll leave you to find your bearings for a few minutes, but don't go wandering off where I can't see you.' With that, she reached back inside the car and pulled out the rubber mat I'd had my 'mishap' on. I heard her mutter something about scrubbing the mat (and her shoe) with hot, soapy water, as well as having to spray the floor with disinfectant. 'God help us!' she gagged. 'No wonder I spewed!'

I didn't let on I'd heard, of course, although I felt aggrieved, hurt even, at having my own efforts at cleaning up pooh-poohed in such an insensitive way. But I let the incident pass, realising that it had only been one of those differences in standards I told you about: little dissimilarities that would become apparent between us from time to time. She was doing her best, and I gave her due credit for that. Not a problem. I mean, the way I looked at it, if she wanted to waste her time re-doing work that had already been done, it was no skin off my nose – to borrow one of your more curious expressions.

Which prompts me to remind you that only the thoughts expressed here are mine, while the words are entirely those of the human being who's attempting to translate them into a form you can understand. By the same token, it may also be a good idea for me to cease referring to the Boss's wife as the Lady Bitch, mindful as I am that, despite my earlier assurances, the use of that particular moniker still risks causing offence to the less open-minded of you. I think it's best, therefore, that I simply call her 'Lady B' from now on.

Now then, what was I talking about? Oh yes, my first impressions of Cuddy Neuk…

Like I said before, I took to it straight away. And it wasn't just the look of the place either, for I was equally impressed by the location. The little farmstead was set on the brow of gently rising land that rolled away over neat, walled-in fields and patches of woodland stepping all the way down to the sea, a mile or so to the north. I had seen the sea before, right enough, but it had been from a long way off, up in the hills at old Doddie's. From there, the views were so often blurred by mist and low cloud that any glimpse of sea you did manage to snatch had the appearance of a hazy extension of the sky. To be honest, I usually had to strain my eyes to make out any hint of horizon at all. And that's saying something, coming from a Border collie, a breed of dog renowned for its sharpness of vision. Oh, by the way, you should hear old Doddie holding forth about *that* when he's in full pup-selling flow…

'See them dugs o' mine? Well, there's no another type o' creetchur in the whole actual animal kingdom that has eyesight as keen as them. Fair phenonimo it is.' He'd then be liable to point to the far horizon (or the lack of horizon I've just been telling you about) and say, 'Aye, if them dugs o' mine could talk, they'd be able tae tell ye what brand o' fag a man standin' on yon hillside was smokin'. OK, fair enough, Ah know ye might think it's uncanny, seein' as how the hills we're lookin' at are maybe upward o' thirty mile away, but it's still a fac' for a' that. Oh, yes indeed, a braw sense o' sight, them dugs o' mine. Could spot a sheep hidin' doon a coalmine wi' the lights oot. Damn right. Nah, nah, never been any crafty auld yowe could pull the wool ower *their* eyes. Tellin' ye!'

But there I go digressing again. To be frank, if I have a fault at all it's that I tend to drift away from the point sometimes. I know I do – especially recently. Anyway, what I was about to say was that the sea was now near enough for me to actually smell it for the first time ever. And I'll tell you this: it gave me a feeling of pleasure that I've never forgotten. Don't get me wrong – there was nothing bad about the air up on old Doddie's hillsides. Far from it. Indeed, the scents of heather and whin and the countless other wild plants and flowers you only find in the hills were a joy, even when tinged with the ever-present whiff of sheep, deer and grouse droppings. In all fairness, though, the subtle smell of those 'animal deposits' (doubtless more apparent to dogs than humans) actually blended well with the other aromas I mentioned. They were all component parts of the character of the hills: *natural* things that a nature girl like myself feels at one with.

Yet the atmosphere at Cuddy Neuk, infused as it was with the faint, salty tang of the sea, was like a breath of fresh air to me. Literally. It's hard to explain, but it somehow made me feel more *alive* than I'd ever felt before. Like the air, I was infused with a kind of, I don't know, 'sparkliness' – *joie de vivre* you'd probably call it – and it appealed to me. A lot.

While I was standing there with my nose in the air, savouring every sniff of this new sensation, the wind changed slightly, and I became aware of an all-too-familiar aroma drifting into my nostrils. 'Surely not!' I thought. But a collie's nose is nothing if not reliable, so I instinctively knew that mine wasn't playing tricks on me now. I turned my head into the breeze, and sure enough, there they were, blissfully nibbling their way over the crown of a grass field on the other side of the road. 'Bugger! And I thought I'd seen the last of sheep when I came here!'

But the Lady Bitch – sorry, Lady B – was about to reveal that she was more perceptive than she looked. And I say this with no intention of suggesting that I'd taken her to be in any way dim-witted. Not at all. It was simply that I'd assumed that any human's powers of observation would be similar to old Doddie's, and he was about as visually alert as a bat. I could give you examples, and I may – if I feel like it – but not now. That would send me off at a tangent again, and I'm making a conscious effort to avoid that if I possibly can.

Now, where was I again? Oh yes, that was it. I was going to tell you about Lady B and the unexpected appearance of a bunch of sheep at the supposedly sheepless Cuddy Neuk.

'Don't worry, Jen,' she said when she noticed me staring wide-eyed across the road, 'they're not ours, so you won't be sent to round them up or anything.' She then proceeded to explain that the sheep, and the field they were grazing in, belonged to a neighbouring farmer. Jack, she called him – a nice old man, and a good friend, who owned a lot of sheep, and sheepdogs too – collies – three of them – all good workers, well up to looking after his sheep without any *assistance* from me. 'And besides,' she said, 'you're not to go near that road anyway. It's dangerous. Cars and lorries coming far too fast round the corner near our entrance there.' She patted my head again. 'So there you are – the two rules of your new home: keep away from the road and don't go bothering Jack's sheep.'

I could see what she meant about the road. Cars were going past at quite a lick, although they *were* fairly few and far between. Even so, there were more than enough of them for my liking, considering I'd spent all of my life up to then in the back of beyond, where we never saw a motor vehicle of any kind for days on end, and even then it was usually just the postie's van going at snail's pace over the bumps and potholes in the track leading up to old Doddie's house. There was no danger posed to man or beast by traffic up there.

In actual fact, the first traffic, if you can call it traffic, I'd ever seen had been one car, a pick-up truck and a tractor making their leisurely way through the village of Gifford not long after we'd set out from Doddie's place that afternoon. I just happened to be feeling a wee bit travel sick at the time, though, so didn't take much notice of the motorised aspect of Gifford. Or any other aspect of Gifford for that matter, despite Lady B blethering on about how pretty it was and how it was a favourite haunt of local hill farmers and shepherds like old Doddie, and how that pub there was where they all usually gathered and got plastered (whatever that meant) every Saturday night, although some of them preferred that other pub there. I know she was only trying to make me take an interest in all these aspects of the wider world I was now entering into, but I honestly didn't feel up to listening to any of it just then. As I say, I was feeling a bit poorly and, quite frankly, I really couldn't have cared less about what she was chattering on about anyway. I mean, what interest is a quaint little church here and an old-fashioned village post office there to a pedigree Border collie, for heaven's sake? But all the same, I knew she was only doing her best. Actually, I had already noticed that she was *always* trying to do her best, and I liked that. I mean, you'll probably remember I made that point about my two brothers: you know, about how they worked hard at learning to work sheep, always doing their best to please old Doddie, even showing off to him like idiots while he was busy trying to flog me to Lady B. No, honestly, I really liked that about my two brothers. I honestly did. Sometimes.

But that aside, when we arrived in the market town of Haddington a wee while later (I had thrown up by now, by the way, so was feeling pretty much my old self again), I was introduced to *real* traffic for the first time ever, and the sight, sound and smell of it almost made me throw up again. I kid you not. What I did, though, was to stop looking out the window and concentrate on looking at Lady B's elbow instead. And if you're wondering why I picked on her elbow, it's because it moved a lot less suddenly than that foot of hers on the pedal thing, and I needed something to concentrate on that wouldn't make me regurgitate my Wilson's Dog Meal again. That's another thing about us collies: not only are we super-intelligent, we're also very good at thinking our way coolly and calmly out of tricky situations by concentrating on things like elbows, while lesser breeds would keep gaping out at the traffic until they puked.

So, I'd have no problem following Lady B's advice about the road next to Cuddy Neuk. I'd already made my decision about keeping cars out of my life anyway, as I think I mentioned before. But keeping away from sheep – well, that was a different matter entirely. The thing was, while I was dead against being forced to *work* with sheep, I really enjoyed having fun with them, and I'd learned that they liked having fun with me too. OK, I admit not all of them enjoyed a game of 'Tig' like those two orphan lambs I told you about, but even the older ones I'd sent scattering all over the hillside appreciated the taste of freedom I'd given them, and they wouldn't have had that taste of freedom if I hadn't defied all orders to the contrary. It was all a product of having fun, and I had a hunch farmer Jack's sheep would also be up for a caper when the time came.

But the time wasn't now. Lady B had set the ground rules, and I had no intention of breaking them. Not until I had settled in properly at any rate – and even then I'd make sure it was on the q.t. The thing is, patience is a virtue, and that's another quality collies have in abundance. How else do you think they can bear lying about for ages in a fly-ridden clump of heather waiting for a huddle of dozy sheep to make a wrong move? No, the right opportunity to give some of Jack's flock a treat would come round soon enough, but in the meantime I'd behave like the obedient dog my new human partners wanted. Well, as far as my independent nature and freedom of spirit would allow, that's to say.

* * * * *

– THREE –

THE STRANGEST THING happened when I met the Boss for the first time. Lady B had only just finished giving me her pep talk on the dangers of the road and the need for me to resist all temptations to introduce myself to farmer Jack's sheep. She had also pointed out that, unlike the boundless expanses of the Lammermuir Hills I'd been accustomed to, the land hereabouts was divided into distinct fields, with those beyond our own boundaries belonging to neighbours, who wouldn't necessarily welcome an uninvited 'guest dog' on their land. I was still in the process of trying to adjust my mindset to this unexpected curb on my freedom when a tractor came chugging into the yard.

'Time to meet the Boss,' Lady B told me, then added with a wily wink, 'Well, we like to let him *think* he is, anyway.'

The tractor's cab door opened and down jumped a tallish young man wearing work-soiled dungarees and a broad smile. 'Well, well, well,' he said to Lady

B, 'who have we got here?'

She glanced down at me with a look of self-congratulation, reminding me of an old ewe that had just given birth to triplets. 'This is Jen, bought at a bargain price from old Doddie's school of champion sheepdogs, where she earned top marks in ... well, in being a *free spirit*, according to the principal himself.'

The Boss gave a little laugh, the type of laugh that said he approved of what he had been told, and with a glint in his eye that said he also approved of what he was looking at. And it can honestly be said the feeling was entirely mutual. I liked the look of this human. We were on the same wavelength, and I instinctively knew, as with my initial inkling about Lady B, that we'd get along just fine. All dogs of any intelligence, but collies in particular, are able to judge a human's character in an instant. Don't ask me how. It's just a gift of nature, I suppose – something that's in us, and I've never seen the need to think more deeply about it than that.

What I did do then, though, was make a quick comparison between the Boss and old Doddie, with particular regard to the training of dogs and the bearing this might have on my future in terms of what could loosely be called 'work'. You may recall old Doddie's golden rule was that, to successfully train a dog, the human had to establish early doors that he was smarter than the dog; that the trainer had to have, in his words, 'more between the lugs' than the trainee. Of course, it hadn't taken me long to figure out – and prove – that this assertion became no more than a puff of hot air wafting over the hillside when the trainee turned out to have appreciably 'more between the lugs' than the trainer.

Drawing from this experience, I swiftly appraised the Boss's potential as a dog trainer, and came to the conclusion that it would be, in all probability, on the debit side of mediocre, at least when having his wits pitted against mine. And this wasn't because I judged him to be less intelligent than I was – not *particularly* so at any rate – but rather because I sensed that he regarded me as a creature of no less worth than himself. Here at last was a human who thought my way, and I liked his attitude.

So, there I was, standing opposite the Boss with this favourable judgement of his character already established in my mind, when this strange thing happened: the strange thing I mentioned a bit earlier...

'Hello, Jen,' he grinned. 'Well, you're a *right* bonnie lass, aren't you?' He sort of bent forwards a little and beckoned me to go to him. 'Come on – come and say hello. I won't bite you.'

Why he said that, I don't know. Maybe he thought I looked a bit nervous and was trying to make me feel at ease. But even though I wasn't feeling in the slightest nervous, I started to do something that may have given the impression that I was. It was something I'd never done before. Very strange. And to make it even stranger, I did it automatically, unintentionally, yet probably appearing to the onlooker as if it was what I *normally* did on such occasions. What I found myself doing was sort of crouching down, while creeping towards the Boss. All right, I know it would have looked absolutely normal if I had been trying to put the hypnotic fix on a mob of wayward sheep, but when introducing myself to a human who regarded me as an equal being ... well, that didn't show me up in the right light at all.

And as if that weren't weird enough, I also found myself smiling an involuntary smile, with the lip of one side of my mouth raised to reveal a perfectly spaced line of razor sharp teeth. It was the type of snarly face I'd make to warn my brothers to back off, to stop bothering me, if they were acting like idiots, which they usually were, except when trying to impress old Doddie with their working 'talents'. But I wasn't trying to put the frighteners on the Boss. Quite the opposite, and fortunately for me he seemed to realise it.

'Well, that *is* a lovely smile you've got there, Jen,' he said, smiling himself. 'But, hey, no need to *coorie doon* like that. I won't hurt you.' He popped his fingers a few times and added reassuringly, 'Come on – come and say hello.' Then he did what I would later learn was what many humans do when they want a dog to come to them: he gently patted his chest with the palm of one hand. 'Come on now – there's a good girl.'

Apparently, some people choose to convey the same message by patting their knees, but I knew nothing of such odd practices back then. So, taking the Boss at his word, I duly launched myself upward towards his chest and, for some inexplicable reason, performed a simultaneous back flip to land belly-up like a helpless baby in his arms.

'Wow, neat trick, lass!' he laughed. 'Where'd you

learn that one?'

I wasn't familiar with the word 'trick' at the time, so didn't realise how inappropriate it was when related to a dignified young lady like me. Consequently, I showed no reaction, though taking the precaution of committing the word to memory for future reference.

But for the moment, I actually felt quite chuffed with myself. Clearly, the Boss had been favourably impressed by my impromptu display of acrobatic agility, and Lady B added to my elation by grinning broadly while stepping forward to 'tickle my tummy', as she said. I hadn't experienced that sensation before, but I liked it. A lot.

'She obviously puts a huge amount of trust in your ability to catch her in mid air,' she told the Boss. 'A lot more than I would!'

It crossed my mind that it might well have knocked the Boss flat on his back if Lady B *had* tried the same stunt, but I stifled the notion. She *was* quite slim, after all, and couldn't help it if her human frame wasn't as well suited to such acts of nimbleness as a collie's. But then she made a remark which I found somewhat demeaning and hurtful.

'*Phew*!' she sniffed, swiftly withdrawing her tickling fingers as if she had just touched a stinging nettle. 'You're a wee bit pongy, aren't you, pet? Fur a bit matted too. Hmm, a bath is called for, methinks.'

'Not a bit of it,' the Boss chuckled as he placed me back on all fours. 'She's fine. Let her settle in a while before you think of anything like baths.' He ruffled my head. 'You smell nice, don't you, Jen? Just the way a working dog should.'

There were two elements to that statement: one I agreed with, while the other I took exception to. I most certainly did smell nice, a lot nicer than Lady B and all that fake-flowery scent of hers, but I wasn't at all happy about being called a *working* dog. As much as my initial impressions of the Boss had been good, I realised then that, if our future relationship was to get off to a positive start, I'd have to make an effort to enlighten him on my proper function in life. But not a problem. I was well up to the task.

Then Lady B made another comment to the Boss that irked me even more than her previous one. 'You know, I've been thinking: rolling over on their backs is actually a sign of submission in dogs – showing they feel subservient to you. And I'm sure that'll even apply to the flying version Jen just did.'

What on earth was she talking about? Big words, but it wasn't too difficult to work out what Lady B was driving at. Sub*miss*ive? Sub*ser*vient? *Me*? Oh, no, no, no, I didn't like the sound of this at all. Those descriptions may well have been correctly applied to dogs in general, especially to numpties like those work-happy brothers of mine. But to *me*? No way! But then I thought – hold on a minute here. No point in cutting off my nose to spite my face, to borrow another of those queer expressions humans like to use. Short-lived though it had been, that tickling-my-tummy experience had been really enjoyable. I'd never been treated to such a sensation before, and wouldn't have minded being treated to it again. Soon … and often. And if this whole episode amused the Boss as much as it seemed to, then maybe *pretending* to be submissive occasionally wouldn't be such a bad idea after all. Yes, that was it: I'd adopt the flying back flip as my own special 'trick' and perform it for the Boss every time I felt in need of having my belly rubbed. You bet I would, and if Lady B didn't feel comfortable about doing that little favour for me, I was pretty sure the Boss would be only too pleased to oblige.

So far so good, and the outlook was about to get even brighter...

*

I WAS ALREADY quite used to seeing young animals and birds: lots of lambs, of course, and puppies too, with the occasional baby hare, a few grouse and partridge chicks, and even some ducklings at one of the little ponds you find here and there in the hills. But I hadn't come across young humans, so didn't know what to expect when the Boss and Lady B told me I'd be meeting theirs any minute now. Sure enough, just when all the excitement of my flying back flip had died down, a car drew up at the gate and out clambered two of what the Boss said were 'boys', which I immediately took to be juvenile *males* of the human species. The clue was in the smell, you see. Oh yes, a very interesting point, which I'll return to later. Anyway, the boys came hurrying towards us with expectant grins on their faces.

'That's not a boxer!' objected the smaller of the two, coming to a sudden stop and frowning. He turned to his mother. 'Thought you said we were going to get another dog like Muffet.'

'That's right, and this is her – Jen.'

The boy's frown deepened. 'Doesn't look like Muffet.'

'That's because she's a collie,' said the larger boy, as he knelt down and gave me a hug. He leaned back and smiled at me. 'Yes, and a really bonnie one too, aren't you?'

The Boss patted the smaller boy on the head. 'We told you we were going to get another dog, but that didn't necessarily mean another boxer. Collies are great dogs too, and Jen will be just as good a pal as Muffet was – you'll see.'

The smaller boy looked up at his father, then at me, then at his mother. 'And she'll play with us? Just like Muffet did?'

Lady B tousled his hair. 'You go and give Jen a big cuddle. Let her know you're her friend. She'll never forget it. Believe me.'

The little lad did his mother's bidding, and I licked the smile that was already lighting his face. Then I did the same to his brother. Although I didn't know the meaning of the words 'Muffet' and 'boxer', I could tell from the way the boys were behaving, and from their thoughts more than anything, that they were hoping I might be the one to take the place of a dog that had meant a great deal to them: a dog that I sensed had recently died. That was all I needed to know. Once more, I was well up to the task, and wouldn't let them down – ever.

I sealed the pact by standing on my back legs, draping my forelegs over the boys' shoulders and nuzzling my head against theirs. It was my off-the-cuff attempt to emulate the 'hugs' or 'cuddles' the boys had given me. Although it was a ritual I wasn't familiar with, I'd quickly cottoned on to it being a show of affection on their part, and I couldn't have been more keen to return the compliment.

The Boss and Lady B then introduced me formally to their sons by telling me their human names. But I'd already decided that I would think of them simply as Boy One for the larger of the two, and Boy Two for the smaller. I hadn't a clue about how to tell the age of humans – not in terms of their conception of time anyway – but I found out in due course that Boy One was about seven years of age, while Boy Two was something like two or three years younger. This made me, as a one-year-old collie, about the same age in human years as Boy One, but of course I was already much more advanced mentally than he was. He'd have no cause to worry, though: I'd be careful not to make him feel inferior.

But getting back to the point I made about there being no need for me to be told that 'boys' were males: I said the clue was in the smell, so let me explain...

I've already referred to a dog's amazing sense of smell (particularly a collie's), which I assure you is in a different league from a human's. It's so superior, in fact, that you wouldn't be able to understand the extent of the difference, even if I could put it into words. Which I can't. Nobody can. However, it may help you to appreciate a little better what I'm about to tell you if I say that, to imagine what even an average dog's sense of smell is like, a human would require eyesight to match the optical power that old Doddie claimed for 'his dugs', which was to be able to tell what brand of cigarette a man was smoking on a hillside some thirty miles way. More than that, you'd have no trouble in seeing through his trousers to identify the colour and material of the underpants he was wearing, who might have worn them before him, where he bought them, and how long ago. That puts a dog's sense of smell roughly into context for you.

You can take it, therefore, that I had already formed a fairly comprehensive assessment of the boys' personal details a couple of seconds after they'd alighted from the car. Bear in mind that my only previous experience of any human had been old Doddie, and I had already deduced from my brief contact with the Boss and Lady B that Doddie's smell wasn't typical. Well, to be fair, in one underlying way it was. I'm talking about the *natural* scent of human skin, which a dog can easily distinguish from that of, say, a sheep, or another dog, even when that scent is masked by the likes of Lady B's perfume, hints of tractor fumes on the Boss, or the whiff of sheep dip and pipe tobacco on old Doddie.

But the most obvious clue to the boys' gender was the one odour they *did* share with both Doddie and, to a lesser extent, their father: an odour, crucially, that wasn't apparent on their mother. In short, I had established from the initial waft emanating from the boys that, while they didn't smoke a pipe or work with sheep dip, they *were* prone to indulging in Doddie's most distinguishing habit. Farting.

Yet there remained an element of confusion in my mind as regards the absence of this smell on Lady B. Was its absence common to all human females, or only to Lady B? Or, for that matter, was it merely being overpowered in her case by that fake-floral perfume of hers? There were too many things happening on that first day at Cuddy Neuk for me to give much thought to the matter, but as the years passed and my familiarity with humans increased, the veil of uncertainty gradually lifted.

Now, as I relate this account after a long and informative life, I can categorically assure you that any woman who claims never to have dropped the occasional quiet one in her knickers is not only a unique member of the human race, but is also a truly exceptional mammal. Yes, and women should be aware that those 'silent' ones they let go in company aren't as silent as they think. Not to a dog anyway. And don't try and pass the buck by blaming us either. We know the routine – a demure cough behind your hand, while casting an accusing glance at the family pet. Talk about devious! But the truth is out, ladies. You've been rumbled, and you can count yourselves lucky if the next dog you try and frame has the good grace not to reveal all by standing in front of you, nose in the air, sniffing, then howling in distress.

But there I go digressing again. Let's see, I was talking about my first meeting with Boy One and Boy Two, wasn't I? That's right, and what I was going to tell you was that we clicked immediately. You see, they made no attempt to disguise the fact that enjoying themselves was their priority in life, and just in case I might have been in any doubt about it, they wasted no time in inviting me to have some fun.

'Game of football, Jen?' beamed Boy One. 'Know how to play football, do you?'

'Let's go, Jen!' chirped Boy Two, clapping his hands together and nodding towards a large area of neatly mowed grass at the side of the house. 'Come on ... you can be on my team!'

I'd never heard of football, but it didn't take me long to learn the basics. Actually, I'm being over modest again. To be absolutely honest, a few seconds watching the boys play for my benefit was all I needed to fully grasp the rules. Pretty simple, really. And considering I'd never even seen a football up to then, I can claim without fear of contradiction that I showed in a flash that I was a natural player, being much better suited physically to mastering the required skills than the boys themselves.

I mean, I twigged right away that the idea was to use your feet to control the ball. Hence the term 'football'. OK, I got that easily enough. Also, I quickly gathered from the boys' demo that the object of the game was to get the ball away from the other player and run away with it. And if you managed to take the ball up to one end of the 'pitch', as they called it, one player jumped up and down, flung his arms in the air and yelled with joy, while the other slouched around mumbling to himself. Pretty pointless, I suppose, but the boys enjoyed it, and the sense of fun was infectious.

So, I got stuck into the action with a vengeance and immediately showed how being a dog gave me a distinct advantage over humans. You see, while they were limited to controlling the ball with their two feet (Boy One told me 'dribbling' was the technical term for this manoeuvre), I was able to use four feet *and* my nose to achieve the same result. As you can imagine, I dribbled better than they did, and a lot faster too.

You should have seen me go! Honestly, I was so fast I almost surprised myself, and not only when going in a straight line either. The thing is, I quickly got bored of dribbling the ball up to one end of the pitch and then the other. And the boys weren't skilled enough to do anything about it, even though I let them join forces to 'team up' against me. That's when I really started running rings round them, dribbling the ball between their legs then heading off at speed to leave them floundering about on the ground. More than that, I did all this while keeping up an incessant barrage of barking. No wonder the boys were impressed. Fair enough, I knew I wasn't playing by the same rules they had sketched out for me at the kick-off, but it was for their own long-term good to learn that there wasn't a rule yet made that I couldn't or wouldn't break. Still, I had to give both of them credit for taking it all in good part. They even stood and cheered every time I won the ball and darted away to 'score' at whichever end of the pitch I fancied.

'*FOUL*!', they roared, or '*CHEAT*! *PENALTY*!'.

Yes, they were *really* good sports, the boys, and very magnanimous in defeat as well.

'You're some dog, Jen,' Boy One puffed as the

three of us lay panting on the grass at the end of the game. 'Muffet never played that way!'

'No, and – and anyway,' little Boy Two chipped in between gasps, 'I thought you were supposed to be on *my* side!'

Well, I could understand that the wee chap was a bit disappointed, but taking both boys on at once had been my way of trying to even things up for them: to redress the imbalance of pitting human against collie, you could say. Anyhow, I gave his face a big lick to let him know I hadn't taken offence at his remark. After all, he *was* very young and obviously had a lot to learn about football … and collies.

* * * * *

– FOUR –

THE 'LOVE' WORD isn't too often used by Scottish country folk. They seem to think it's a bit slushy, corny even. Again, I've learned this through years of watching and listening. And it's a trait I could identify with, because collies don't readily forge or make a show of affectionate relationships either. Not this collie anyway, and I'm sure I'm not unique. I mean, we really have to be sure we actually *like* someone before we even accept an invitation to step closer for a pat on the head. Believe me, many are the occasions I've completely ignored such an overture, especially when too gushingly made...

'Oooh, look at you! What a nice doggy. Give me a nice paw, nice doggy, and I'll give you a nice pat on the head.'

Nice pat on the head, my arse! No, if the thought waves weren't right, that was that. All the same, I have to confess that maybe part of the problem was that I didn't quite understand the true meaning of the 'love' word, which harked back to my formative period with old Doddie and his rare use of it – always when talking to himself, of course.

'Man, man, Doddie,' he'd say on a summer's day, after sitting on a rock for hours watching his flock graze in a sun-parched glen, 'Ah'd really *love* a cold beer!' Then, on a similar occasion, he'd be just as liable to mutter, 'Christ, Ah could *murder* a fuckin' pint!'

No wonder I was confused.

And that's probably why I had never given the matter much thought until my first night at Cuddy Neuk. Even then, it took a while for it to come to mind, since I'd had so many other new experiences to consider, not least of which was the way I was being regarded by the little group of humans that fate had singled out for me to look after. By the time darkness fell, I was already confident that I had won over the Boss and the two boys. They clearly thought I was fantastic, as I had more or less predicted when we were introduced. No great surprise there. But as much as I knew Lady B and I had also taken to each other the moment we met at the side of old Doddie's lambing shed, a few nagging doubts about her attitude towards me had since crept into my mind. I'm now referring in particular, as you may have guessed, to the comment she made to the Boss about me being 'a wee bit *pongy*'. You'll doubtless recall that she also suggested I might need a bath. A *bath* of all things!

It came as something of a shock, therefore, when Lady B ushered me into the house in front of her. Just think of it: me, a 'pongy' young sheepdog, who had previously spent all of her nights with miscellaneous canine relations in a scruffy, mouse-infested shack in the hills, being invited into a proper human house. Yes, and one that was home to the most pernickety of human females at that. (Thoughts of her dismissive attitude towards my efforts to clean the floor of her car after my little 'mishap' were still fresh in my mind. And it rankled slightly.)

'It's getting chilly, Jen,' she said. 'In you come and keep cosy by the fire.'

Cosy? By the *fire*? Was I hearing things? A human being showing concern for my creature comforts when the temperature dropped slightly? I hadn't seen that coming. No, I'd taken for granted I'd be provided with overnight shelter in a little hut like the one at old Doddie's, or maybe even in the barn on the other side of the yard from the house. That's what I fully expected, and it really would have been fine by me. You don't miss what you've never had, after all, and I don't mind admitting I was so taken aback by Lady B's invitation that I stood gawping up at her with what could easily have been mistaken for a gormless look on my face.

'Go on, Jen,' she urged. 'In you go. We're letting the cold in, standing here with the door wide open like this.'

The next few minutes were a bit of a blur: the two boys fussing over me and encouraging me to 'snuggle down' with them on a rug in front of an open fire; Lady B telling them to *stop* fussing over me and give me time to get used to being in the house; the Boss clicking a switch on a wooden box thing in the corner, before slumping down on a couch at one side of the fire, then telling Lady B to stop fussing over the boys and me and settle down beside him; Lady B darting in and out of the room, bringing cups of something warm and sweet-smelling for the boys, a glass of something that looked and smelled like sheep's urine for the Boss, and a bowl of water for me.

All the while, the boys continued to fuss over me, while the Boss kept getting up to stomp over to the wooden box, which he thumped and grumped at until it lit up and tiny humans appeared inside a window on the front. These miniature people started jumping up and down, before disappearing again and causing the Boss to repeat the exercise over and over again until he was satisfied the occupants of the box had finally stopped disappearing for good.

It was pandemonium. But I liked it.

'Nice drop o' lager, this,' said the Boss, comfortably settled on the couch at last and licking his lips while surveying the glass in his hand. 'Could've been a bit colder, though.'

'It *was* cold – *very* cold,' Lady B retorted as she sat down beside him, 'until you spent the past fifteen minutes waging your nightly war with the telly.'

'Yeah,' the Boss nodded absently, 'must get somebody to check it over tomorrow.'

'You've been saying that for six months now.'

The Boss took a slurp from his glass, then surveyed it again, smiling. 'Yeah, nice drop o' lager ... even if it is kinda warm.' He glanced briefly at Lady B. 'Maybe you should set the fridge a bit colder.'

Lady B just sighed and made herself comfortable, as earlier instructed. Finally, an air of tranquillity descended on the room, so I stretched out on my side between the boys, closed my eyes and savoured the warmth of the fire. Ah-h-h, this was living all right.

I must have dropped off soon after, and woke up with a start when the Boss shouted something about the damned telly being ready for the scrap heap. It was the type of thing I'd heard a few times from inside the dog shack when old Doddie left his house door open of an evening. I'd had no idea what the 'telly' thing was he was getting so annoyed at, and I wasn't much wiser now that I'd actually seen one. To me, it was just a wooden box with tiny people moving about inside. Humans never failed to amaze me, getting all hot and bothered about a wooden box with tiny people moving about inside. And sitting staring at it for ages as well. Weird. And when I thought about it, it dawned on me that this must have been what old Doddie had been doing in the evenings as well. Yes, he was always yelling things like, 'Bloody telly! Loada bollocks!' and I used to wonder about the meaning of it all. But it was beginning to make sense now – except the Boss had different words to shout at *his* telly. They *were* all angry-sounding too, though.

I lay and watched the box for a while myself then, just to see if I could get a clue about the strange power it seemed to hold over humans, even the young ones. But I couldn't figure it out. What I did think, though, was that if any of these tiny people escaped out of the box's window, it would be great fun rounding them all up, and I'd be right there, ready and waiting to do just that. But it didn't happen – not that night and never at any other time I've watched the telly in the ensuing years. Thereby lies another tale, however, and I'll tell you about it later … if I remember.

On that first occasion, the boredom of watching the box, combined with the heat from the fire, must eventually have sent me to sleep again. And I had this dream, and in it Lady B was telling the Boss that the heat from the fire was making me pong worse than ever and she had a good mind to fling me in the bath there and then. Well, I *think* it was a dream. See, that's the thing about us dogs – we're really light sleepers. What happens is, we have our eyes closed, but our ears and nose are still switched on and poised to alert us to any danger that might be coming our way. It can be a very useful gift, but can sometimes make us dream something is happening when it isn't, particularly when nothing *is* actually happening, if you see what I mean. What I'm saying is that this sixth sense thing we have when we're sleeping may well have played a trick on my mind about Lady B threatening to fling me in a bath, when she didn't actually say that at all – except in my dream. In any event, that's what I decided had happened when I came to again.

By this time, the boys were being bundled off to bed by their mother, who was firmly rejecting their suggestions that I should go with them. They'd see me again in the morning, she said. No need to worry about that. As for the Boss, he was still slouched by the fire, but sound asleep, his head lolling back, mouth gaping open, and with his glass – empty now – still firmly clasped in his hand. He was snoring, and I detected a muffled '*Pa-a-r-r-rp!*' resonating from the corner of the couch where he was sitting. It seemed

Lady B had caught wind of it too. Literally.

'There you are, Jen,' she said po-faced while nodding sideways in his direction. 'The Boss ... alias Prince Charming. I wonder how long it'll be before he turns back into a frog!'

Now, far be it from me to suggest there may have been an element of wishful thinking in her words, because I really was getting nothing from all quarters of the family but good thought waves, or 'vibes' as you'd probably call them. All the same, I did have a feeling that the Boss maybe did try Lady B's patience at times, certainly in terms of his relationship with the telly and that sheep's urine stuff he seemed to guzzle with relish – if tonight's proceedings were anything to go by, that's to say.

'Anyway, time for those of us still awake to go to bed,' Lady B told me. 'Come on – I'll show you to your new quarters.' She shepherded me back to the door we'd originally entered the house by, opened it and led me through. Here we go, I thought, loafing by the fire had been an unexpected luxury, but now back to the real world and the doghouse that awaits. However, instead of shooing me off to my new abode, Lady B just stood outside the door, looked at me expectantly and said, 'Go on then – do your business – last chance you'll get till morning.'

Do my *business*? What the hell was she talking about? *Business*? I didn't do business, for God's sake. I was a bloody collie, not one of those sales rep blokes I'd seen coming to old Doddie's and trying to flog him some super-special new sheep dip or something. 'Smarmy arseholes,' he used to call them. I certainly wasn't one of those. So, at a loss for what to to do next, I just stood there and returned Lady B's look.

She gave a little shiver. 'Go on then – do whatever you usually do last thing at night. And be quick about it, Jen – I'm freezing to death out here!'

That's when I finally got the message. Her shiver was the clue. It happened to me sometimes as well when I needed to 'answer the call o' nature,' as I remembered Doddie politely putting it when giving Lady B his sales pitch. Hadn't she been listening to him? Hadn't she taken in that I didn't 'do my business' in public? Not that it mattered either way, since I wasn't about to lower my standards just because there may have been a breakdown in human communications. Here was a perfect example of their inability to read even the most basic of a dog's thoughts, and I confess to being more than a little disappointed in Lady B for that. I'd expected more of her. I honestly had.

'Well, suit yourself,' she finally huffed. 'You've had your chance, and I'm not standing out here with you any longer.' She stepped back inside the house, turned and stared at me for a few seconds. 'Come on then, or are you gonna stay outside all night?'

For the second time that evening, I found myself gawping at Lady B with what could justifiably have been judged (in another dog) a gormless look on my face. With me, it was rather an expression of my wish to give her time to have second thoughts. Just good manners, really. But when she made to close the door on me a moment later, I decided she'd had time enough, and slipped swiftly past her and back inside the house.

'About time,' she said, locking the door. 'Now, come over here with me. I've made you a nice cosy bed.'

That 'cosy' word again, and linked to the 'bed' word now. I was liking the sound of this. And there, tucked away snugly in a corner of the kitchen by a chunky metal box contraption that smelled of burnt wood, was what Lady B had prepared for me. To say I was pleasantly surprised would be putting it mildly, although I was a tad perturbed too. But, conscious as ever of being polite, I made a point of revealing only the positive side of my reaction.

'Aha, I see your tail's wagging again,' smiled Lady B. 'I thought you'd be impressed.' Indicating that I should make myself at home, she showed me where a dish of fresh water had been left next to the back door. It would keep nice and cold there, she assured me, being well away from the wood-burning stove.

With a final wag of my tail, I sat down on my new bed, looked up at her with a smiley face and radiated thought waves of good will and gratitude. That was when she treated me to the biggest surprise of all the pleasant surprises I'd been treated to that day.

'You really are a super dog, Jen,' she said softly, '– even if you do pong a wee bit.' Then, before I'd had a chance to feel properly piqued by what could well have been considered an unnecessary afterthought, she added another, which more than compensated: 'But we love you to bits. We do – really and truly.'

So, *that* was what the 'love' word was all about: a surprise compliment, quickly followed by a sobering slap on the face, then a heart-melting declaration of affection. Humans! They drive me crazy. Neither one thing nor the other. I mean, how can you *love* something to *bits*? As limited as my vocabulary was back then, I knew the coupling of those particular words just didn't make any sense at all. But then Lady B swept all my confusion aside by doing something even more surprising, and this time leaving me in no doubt about its meaning...

'Now,' she said, 'time to say goodnight. You've had a busy day,' she yawned, before adding with a wry smile, 'We both have!'

At that, she knelt down and kissed me on the head. Well, OK, to be absolutely honest, not quite *on* the head, more sort of above it. Quite a bit above it, to be fair. But I didn't care: the thought was there, and that was all that mattered. How amazing! Think about it – me, old Doddie's 'thick-in-the-heid' wee collie bitch, not just *loved* by humans, but loved to bits by them as well. Unbelievable!

I could tell by the way Lady B glanced back at me as she left the kitchen that she knew how thrilled I was. She was reading my thoughts perfectly, and I felt a tinge of remorse for having doubted her ability to do so when urging me to 'do my business' in the yard. I was still contemplating that episode a few moments later, when I overheard Lady B talking quietly to the Boss about it in the hallway...

'Anyhow,' she was saying, 'you'll be pleased to know she's now nicely settled down for her first night in the house. But I'll tell you this, if she pees on the kitchen floor tonight, she may well have shit in her own nest for the first time – *if* we're to believe her esteemed breeder – but it'll also be the last!'

Yet again she had strung together a statement of contradictions, which I decided to leave till another time to try and figure out. All I wanted for the present was to savour the feeling of unconditional love that Lady B had conveyed on behalf of my new family. I also wanted to enjoy the luxury of having my own bed, unbothered by the pushing, shoving, kicking and growling of my hitherto bedmates, as well as the squeaking and scratching of the resident tribe of doghouse mice.

But there was a snag, namely the 'perturbing' thing I touched on earlier. Although I hadn't given any indication to Lady B, I had a problem with the bed she'd prepared for me. I could see she had done her best, which I'd already identified as being a prominent characteristic of hers, and covering my bed in an old sheepskin rug would have been her way of doing her best to make me feel at home. However, no matter how much I had delighted in having a caper with old Doddie's sheep, I'd always had respect for them, and lying down to sleep on the remnants of a dead one wouldn't have shown much evidence of that. Besides, the heat from that old wood burner she'd placed my bed beside soon became unbearable. When you're accustomed to sleeping in an airy environment (and old Doddie's ramshackle doghouse was nothing if not airy) you don't take easily to an ultra-cosy little nest like the one I'd been assigned in the Cuddy Neuk kitchen. That being the case, I took myself over to the back door and curled up on the knobbly rubber doormat. Perfect! A good firm 'mattress' that reminded me of the knotty wooden floor in the old shack, and a cooling draft drifting under the door to replicate the natural 'air conditioning' I was accustomed to back there as well.

And, I mused as I drifted off, an additional bonus of this move would be that, in the morning, Lady B would take one look at the neat, unruffled state of the sheepskin rug and maybe give me another kiss on the head for being such a neat and tidy dog. I mean, I'd already had ample experience of how big a cleanliness freak she was, so why not play to her weaknesses?

* * * * *

– FIVE –

AS WITH THE early part of my initiation as a resident of the Cuddy Neuk farmhouse, my first morning started off with a burst of pandemonium, although of a more frantic nature than the night before. Everyone seemed to be dashing about in different directions, getting in each other's way, mumbling and being shirty. Well, no, on second thoughts, that's not quite true – not the being shirty bit anyway. That activity was limited to the two adults, while their boys, after a brief resumption of making a fuss of me and taking turns at visiting the bathroom, got on with stuffing their faces at the breakfast table.

'Must've been that last can of lager,' moaned the Boss, rubbing his forehead with one hand while rummaging about in a wall cupboard with the other. 'Where's the bloody paracetamols?'

'Must've been that last can of lager, my foot!' stated Lady B, brushing past en route to the table with a bowl of something that reminded me of the 'mishap' I'd had in the car the previous day. 'The damage was done with the first six you downed!'

'Nah, something about that last one. Didn't taste right. Must've been off.'

'Hmm, where have I heard *that* before? And in any case, nobody forced you to drink it, so come and have your porridge – get some nourishment into you – you've a lorry to load this morning.'

The Boss took a quick look at the bowl, retched and continued his quest for pain relief. 'No thanks – can't face it – stomach's really giving me gyp.'

Lady B smirked. 'Oh, yes? Stomach transferred itself up to your head again, has it? One of these times it'll stay there.' She gave a little chuckle, then turned to me and smiled a kindly smile. 'Poor Jen. We've been neglecting you, haven't we? Very inconsiderate of us, and you being such a good girl all night, too.'

That's when I expected her to make a belated gesture of affection related to the neat and tidy sheepskin rug on my bed. But if she'd noticed it at all, she didn't let on. Instead, she patted my head and said, 'A nice clean floor. Clever girl. Yes, and you not even house trained or anything.'

House trained? What was she talking about this time?

Suddenly, she clapped a hand to her cheek as if she'd just thought of something shocking. Wheeling round to face the boys, she blurted out, 'I take it you two let Jen out to do her business when you came through here first thing this morning?'

Little Boy Two's mouth was too full to speak. 'Nope. Forgot all about that,' replied Boy One through a spray of corn flakes. 'Too busy playing with her.'

An apologetic look came to Lady B's face as she

crouched down and held my head between her hands. 'Oh, you poor wee thing,' she crooned. 'You must be absolutely bursting by now. Come on – I'll take you out myself. Those bad boys, eh!'

Take me out? Big deal! What about that kiss I was expecting? That's what I wanted to know.

'Save yourself the bother,' the Boss grunted at lady B. He checked his watch. 'That lorry's gonna be here soon. Jen can come with me – have a rake about the hay shed while I'm loading the bales.'

'Good of you to offer.' Lady B came back. She was getting into a bit of a tizz now, scraping the Boss's uneaten porridge into a bin, clearing the breakfast table, making sure the boys' clothes were neat and tidy, their ears clean. She checked her own watch. 'Look at the time! If the boys don't leave now, they'll miss the school bus. And I've a huge pile of ironing to do – mostly your shirts, as usual. And then I'll have to go down to Haddington to pick some things up at the dry cleaners.' She paused to tickle me under the chin. 'So, on you go with the Boss, Jen. Be a good girl and I'll see you later.'

Still no kiss on the head, though. Ah well, at least she was showing her affection in other ways. Also, in all fairness, she *was* busy, and doing her best under the circumstances – as ever. I really appreciated that. I honestly did. If only she'd stop making such a big thing about me 'doing my business'. Hell's bells, I'd do what I had to do where and when it suited *me* – not anyone else. I began to ask myself if maybe I'd been a bit too quick to give her credit for learning to read my thoughts.

But the Boss's voice jolted me out of my musings. 'Let's go, Jen. I'll show you around while we wait for the lorry.'

IT WAS A bright and brisk autumn morning, with that invigorating hint of sea air adding a sparkle to the atmosphere even more noticeably than it had the previous afternoon. I felt on top of the world. The Boss continued to talk (mutter would be more like it) as we crossed the yard. I noticed he mentioned my name occasionally, so I assumed he was talking to me. Although unable to understand everything he was saying, I did notice the 'lager' word kept cropping up – also 'bloody paracetamols', whatever he meant by that. Anyway, I enjoyed listening to him, and just as well too, because such one-way conversations were to become a regular feature of my relationship with the Boss from that day on. Even if he was only walking past me outside the house or somewhere, he always had a few words to say to me as he went by, sometimes without even looking my way. OK, I don't deny the casual observer might have assumed he was talking to himself. You'll recall I already mentioned that old Doddie had a habit of doing something similar, except in his case he really *was* talking to himself. With the Boss it was different, though, and I knew he was speaking to me, because he said my name, like I told you. But all that aside, it just so happens that there has never been anyone else around on these occasions anyway, so the opinion of casual observers hadn't been worth bothering about in the first place.

As I say, on that first morning he seemed to be

talking mainly about that lager stuff, and it got me wondering again why anyone would want to drink something that smelled like sheep's urine, and looked like it too. Humans never fail to amaze me, drinking stuff that smells like sheep's urine. That said, I do remember one of my brothers used to eat sheep's shit, though only after the sheep had been fed a certain kind of pellets. He seemed drawn to their taste, although I wouldn't have put them anywhere near my own mouth. They had a sort of *unnatural* smell to me, a bit like the vet's car I'm lying beside here. Anyhow, eating those pellets didn't appear to do my brother any harm, though it did make his breath smell funny – sort of like chemical-tainted sheep shit, I suppose.

So there we are: maybe it's not just humans that are a bit weird in this respect. I'm thinking now about something Boy One told his little brother when they came home from school one day. It was haymaking time, and I was sitting in the field with them, watching the Boss towing the reaper behind his tractor. All of a sudden, a rabbit hopped out of the long grass just as the reaper blade was about to demolish its hiding place. The incident prompted Boy One to repeat something his teacher had told him: that rabbits actually eat some of their own droppings as a means of double-digesting their food. Boy Two didn't believe him. He told Boy One he was talking crap, which prompted Boy One to tell him not to use bad language at his age. He'd have to wait until he moved up from infant class at school to be old enough for that. He'd have to be six at least. Wise words indeed from a seven-year-old.

Which brings me to the subject of swear words, and why they slip into my narrative at times. I'm very aware their inclusion may offend some of the more 'sensitive' of you – no doubt the same people who would have taken umbrage at my referring to the Boss's wife as the Lady Bitch – but I'd like to remind you that what is being conveyed here is but an impression of my thoughts, converted into words for your benefit by a human interpreter.

All words are basically just sounds to dogs anyway, and 'shit' doesn't sound all that different from 'sit', so you can hardly blame the dog if you command it to sit by your side and its response is to present you with a rather unpleasant surprise. Words are just sounds, and even when we've learned a fair collection of them over the years, we still don't understand how one can be offensive when one that's almost identical isn't. You see, the fact of the matter is that dogs don't need swear words, and probably wouldn't use them even if they had the 'power' of human speech. Mark you, that's not to say we don't produce thought waves that would turn the air blue at times. And it can all be done with a look. If you don't believe me, pay careful attention to your faithful pooch next time you chastise him unfairly, like when he shits on the carpet just because you didn't pronounce 'sit' distinctly enough. The look he'll give you will accuse you of being an arsehole – or even a fucking moron – more succinctly than words ever could.

But the swear words the Boss was using on that first morning were pretty mild compared to my last example. The truth is that the Boss doesn't really swear much in any case. Well, not in front of the boys and Lady B anyway, and then only the *really* mild ones, like 'damn', 'bloody' and 'hell'. And actually, although she probably wouldn't like to admit it, I've heard Lady B coming out with a couple of those on occasion as well. The boys too; particularly Boy One who, even at only seven years of age, took delight in giving vent to some pretty foul language when any of his school chums came to play. All his pals swore like troopers, and I assumed it was just the young humans' way of showing off to their peers, the way my brothers did with all their idiotic diving about and barking. The only difference was that my brothers actually made a point of doing it in front of old Doddie, whereas the boys were extremely careful *not* to when their parents were about.

But there I go heading off at a tangent again, so I'd better get back to where I was the morning the Boss and I were waiting for that lorry to arrive...

'THAT'S THE OLD byre there,' he said as we crossed the yard from the house. 'It's where we rear the young calves. And over there's the barn – store for all the animal feed and stuff like that. Keep your eyes peeled for mice in there, by the way.' He went on to point out the former stable, which served as a bull pen these days; the old cart sheds, now used for storing implements; and finally, a short distance beyond the yard, a large modern building that housed the older cattle in winter, but was presently stacked high with bales of hay. 'That's where I'll be working this morning, Jen,' he muttered, kneading his brow, 'when that bloody lorry arrives ... and I wouldn't be heartbroken if it didn't!'

From there, he led the way up a nearby incline from where there was an uninterrupted outlook towards the sea, and at right angles to that a view that he said took in most of the Cuddy Neuk land, including a small part of the distant hill field, where the older cattle were currently grazing. He'd take me up there to introduce me to 'the beasts' one day soon, he promised – just to give me a chance to learn a wee bit about their characters before they came in for the winter. I was tempted to think there might have been something slightly ominous in the way he'd said that, but I nipped the notion in the bud. How could cattle be any more of a problem for me than sheep? That's the way I looked at it. And another thing: why was he calling that field the 'hill field'? Even from here, I could see it was nothing but a pimple compared to the *real* hills I was used to. Same went for the extent of the Cuddy Neuk land. Fifty acres, the Boss said. *Fifty*! I admit I knew even less about numbers than I did about words at the time, but my eyes told me the whole of Cuddy Neuk could have been lost in just one of old Doddie's glens. Hell's bells, I'd be able to patrol this patch with one eye closed while still half asleep!

'Now then, Jen,' the Boss piped up in what was almost an assertive voice, 'that over there is the boundary with our nearest neighbours.' He was indicating a hawthorn hedge just a few strides from where we were standing. 'Don't be nipping through there any time you fancy. You're not up in the wide open spaces of the Lammermuir Hills now, you know.'

Lady B had already given me a pep talk on this particular subject, and I had no intention of not doing what I was told. But good intentions and a dedication to freedom were bound to clash sooner or later, and in this instance it proved to be sooner. Almost instantly, in fact.

'There's that damned lorry now,' growled the Boss, nodding towards the farm gate, where a big articulated truck was pulling in from the road. 'Bugger me! Just look at the size of it!' He stomped off, then half turned and shouted, 'You come right behind me, Jen. Don't go wandering in next door there, whatever you do.'

Like I said, I had no intention of disobeying orders, but I wasn't in the habit of meekly obeying them either. And anyway, what was the point of showing me details of my surroundings if I wasn't supposed to make myself properly familiar with them as well? So, as soon as the Boss was out of sight, I headed straight for that boundary hedge he'd been on about and wiggled through the nearest gap. Just another field, I told myself once on the other side. No different from the one I'd just left, except this one had already been ploughed. So what? Made no odds to me.

Then, without warning, I was gripped by one of those little shivers I told you about. You know, the little shivers that suddenly remind you that you need to take a leak. I did need to take one too, and no wonder. I mean, now that I thought about it, I hadn't relieved myself since before I left old Doddie's the previous afternoon. Though totally unaware of it before, I was learning the hard way that it's amazing what moving home can do to upset your regularity. And by the way, I'm not just referring to having a pee either. Nature, to quote old Doddie, was urging me to 'answer her call' without further delay. Which I duly did, in both of the accepted ways, right there beneath our nearest neighbour's hedge. And I freely confess without the slightest tinge of remorse that I've made a habit of doing so every single day in all of the ensuing thirteen years I've lived here.

Have the neighbours complained? Don't be daft! It's a very long hedge, stretching all the way to the so-called hill field, and well out of sight of their farmhouse as well. Aside from all that, it would take an extremely fussy human indeed to go to the bother of singling out my particular deposits among all the fox, rabbit, sparrow and rat shit already there in abundance. Lady B and the Boss had concerned themselves unduly back then, and have lived in blissful ignorance of my private 'business' arrangements ever since.

I KEPT A respectful distance from the Boss's workplace that morning. I'd seen plenty of hay bales before – always being delivered *to* old Doddie's, never being sent away. But I didn't give any thought as to why. You've seen one bale of hay, you've seen them all ... and sheep ate them. That's all I knew, and all I wanted to know. So, instead of following the Boss's suggestion of sniffing about among the bales inside the shed, I lay down outside and watched him loading them onto this huge truck. No kidding, it made you tired just looking at this operation!

He'd placed a long moving ladder sort of contraption between the open front of the shed and the deck of the truck. There was an engine on the side of this machine that somehow made its rungs move constantly upwards, and it was the Boss's job to keep it fed with bales to supply the truck driver, who grabbed them as they arrived at the top and built them layer-upon-layer into an ever-growing stack. It was relentless, back-breaking work for both humans, and I puzzled about why anyone would go to so much trouble to move something so humdrum from one farm to somewhere else – maybe even to the likes of old Doddie's place. As I say, I'd seen hay trucked in for his sheep, so it must have done them *some* good, even if it did taste insipid. I knew what it tasted like because I'd tried it once, just for interest, and I remember thinking only sheep would be daft enough to stand out in the driving snow for hours on end, chewing this stuff with looks of deep satisfaction on their faces. Maybe this particular load *was* actually going to Doddie's as well. I didn't know, and I really didn't care. All I knew was that I was glad I'd been lucky enough to be born a dog.

By the time the load was complete, the big shed was half empty and there was a stack of bales on the platform of the lorry as high and square as a house, all roped down and ready for the road. The Boss and the driver stood leaning against the side of the shed, getting their breath back with the aid of cigarettes. This prompted me to ponder yet again the workings of the human mind. This time I tried to see it their way…

So, you're exhausted and gasping for air after exerting yourself non-stop like an idiot for an hour or two, and the way you help your lungs recover is to take a tube of paper stuffed with dried leaves, stick it in your mouth, set fire to it and inhale the smoke. Sorry, but try as I might I just couldn't make any sense of it. And just think – up to then I'd thought sheep were the stupidest creatures around!

I sidled over and sat by the Boss's side, gazing adoringly up at him. And in case you're wondering, it was a perfectly genuine look too, because I really do like him. A lot. But I'd now seen a side of him that struck me as requiring a bit of sympathy as well, and how better to show sympathy than to adopt the adoring dog look? Incidentally, in case you didn't already know, this is something else that comes naturally to all dogs, and there's none better at it than a Border collie.

'Bonnie-lookin' wee bitch ye've got there, pal,' the truck driver wheezed through belches of cigarette smoke.

'Aye … she is … at that … right enough,' the Boss replied, coughing.

'She'd throw fine pups, ye ken,' the trucker spluttered. 'Aye, get her served while she's young. She'll have a fine big litter in her, and ye'll make yersel a right pile o' money for nothin'.'

Not if I could help it, he wouldn't. Why? Simply because I'd already seen my mother used as a 24-hour filling station by a dozen milk-guzzling pups, including myself. Her undercarriage was head-butted, clawed, yanked-at, gum-sucked, nibbled and gnawed until it was sagging like the seat of old Doddie's jeans on a rainy day. Believe me, I had no desire to put myself through that. Not a chance. I mean, I was justifiably proud of my youthful tits – pert and perfectly formed, all eight of them – and I could see no possible reason for having them permanently disfigured for any human's benefit. Not even the Boss's, much as I liked him.

And while I had no overwhelming reason to *dis*like the truck driver, I can't deny that I wasn't too pleased that he'd taken the liberty of giving the Boss uninvited advice about my reproductive potential right in front of me – almost as if I wasn't there. Rank ignorance and downright bad manners. OK, I wasn't going to dignify his over-familiarity by showing any *immediate* reaction, but I wasn't about to let the episode go without making my feelings felt either.

I waited until he had finished his fag, said his goodbyes to the Boss and started to climb into the cab of his truck. Then, while one of his feet was still on the step, I stretched up and gave him a nip on the heel. It wasn't a full-blooded bite, more a sort of caress with the teeth, but it was enough to let him know that I'd allowed him into my territory on sufferance this time, but if he ever came back, he'd better show more respect. To emphasise the point, I worried the tyre of one of his truck's front wheels all the way down to the gate, barking like fury at the same time. It wasn't a premeditated action, I should stress, just something that came over me on the spur of the moment, and I felt all the better for having done it.

I felt so good, in fact, that I pretty soon employed

the same ritual for seeing off *any* vehicle that was leaving the place, whether driven by friendly visitor, postman, sales rep, baker, butcher, fishmonger or vet. What would immediately puzzle human onlookers was why I worried front tyres instead of the normal collie trait of snapping at the rear ones. Well, where's the skill and bravery in confronting an adversary that's heading *away* from you? Think about it – surely none but the truly fearless have what it takes to stick their head in front of a mass of rolling rubber that could crush you in the blink of an eye.

Anyhow, as he drove off up the road that day, the trucker leaned out of his cab window and shouted back, 'See that dug o' yours, pal – she may be bonnie enough, but she's completely bonkers an' all!'

'*Bonkers*'. I hadn't heard that word before and hadn't the faintest idea of its relevance to the current situation, but I liked the sound of it. Which augured well, because I've heard it applied to me many more times since – purely as a sort of affectionate nickname, I've always reckoned.

'You know, Jen,' said the Boss as he wiped a dribble of sweat from his brow, 'there's an old saying that the best cure for a hangover is a morning of good, hard, honest work. Well, I can tell you from personal experience that whoever said that is an absolute bloody nutcase, and a masochist into the bargain.' He slumped down on some bales, leaned back, closed his eyes and sighed, 'Christ, I could murder a fuckin' pint!'

Now where, I asked myself, had I heard *that* before?

* * * * *

– SIX –

THERE'S SOMETHING ABOUT human laughter that's really uplifting – infectious too, particularly the unrestrained giggles young humans let rip with. I have to confess that this is one form of communication in which the human being has the advantage over us dogs. We can't laugh out loud, simple as that. And it's a real drawback, because we do have a sense of humour and we love having fun, albeit that humans have tried to replace that pleasure with their own work ethic in some of us. It all came about through what they call selective breeding, of course, and although it's probably a very ingenious achievement, I'm no admirer of work for work's sake, as you may already have gathered. And don't kid yourselves, I'm not unique in the dog world either.

Take the wolf, for example. You wouldn't find a wolf working to order for a human, would you? No, and everybody knows we dogs are all really wolves deep down, except most of our wolfie characteristics have been bred out of us down the ages: all the ones humans didn't particularly fancy, at any rate. I mean,

I once saw a little lapdog thing (a Pekinese, I think it was called), and nobody in their wildest dreams could imagine that ball of fluff scaring the living daylights out of a rhinoceros or something, far less hunting it down and eating it. And if you're wondering how I know all this, it's because I've seen it on the telly. But that's another story, and I'll tell you about it later, if you really want to know.

Fine, you may say, but what's all this got to do with a dog's sense of humour? Well, nothing, because I don't suppose wolves could actually laugh out loud any more than their descendants, be they Pekinese or even Border collie. No, I'm just making a point about selective breeding, since I've a few more things to say about that a bit later as well. What I'm saying right now, though, is that we dogs can actually *appear* as if we're laughing. You know the look: mouth open, tongue hanging out, panting, grinning like crazy, eyes gleaming; and to complete this image of unbridled glee, the tail doing its utmost to wag the rest of the dog. What you probably don't realise, though, is that we *are* actually laughing when you see us behaving this way. It's just that we can't make the laughing *sound*, that's all.

But take humans, especially young humans like the ones at Cuddy Neuk for instance, and the sound of laughter you'll hear when they're having fun is the most cheerful sound ever. Honestly, you'd have to be a zombie not to be given a lift by it. It's a bit like the way that hint of sea air affected me on my first morning here. Sparkling is how it made me feel. Sparkling! Yes, and that's how the laughter of young humans makes you feel as well. I promise you, there's no other sound quite like it for raising the spirits ... apart from maybe the song of a blackbird on a summer's evening, or the cheery chirping of a robin on a frosty winter's day.

But still, I think a little kid giggling is my favourite. Dogs have this wonderful affinity with young humans, you see. It's a rapport we don't have with too many adults, and it's easy to understand why. You just have to look at what humans have done to dogs through the ages: using their 'superior intelligence' to alter what nature has provided, in the belief that they're creating something better. Better than the gifts of nature? I don't think so. But that's what happens with kids too, and if you've been lucky enough to spend some time with them before they've been 'tamed' and 'brought to heel', then there's a chance you'll know what I mean. Dogs and little children have a lot more in common than people think. We communicate. That's all I'm saying.

I first realised I could make kids giggle at will one day when I was watching Boy One and Boy Two sitting on a little wall at the side of the yard, idly lobbing stones into an empty tin can – sort of seeing who had the best aim, I suppose the idea was. It didn't seem much like a fun game to me – pretty boring, actually – so I thought I'd spice it up a bit. What I did was, I jumped in and caught one of the stones in mid-flight. Caught it neatly as you like in my mouth. Then I dropped it at the boys' feet and glanced up at them with a look that said, 'OK, let's get some real action going here! You two against me!' They latched on right away – proof of that kid-dog communication thing I just let you in on.

First off, Boy One lobbed a stone, which I intercepted before it reached the can (naturally), then his little brother followed suit, with the same result. You should have heard them laugh! They were having the time of their lives, and I was too, truth to tell – even if the game was so one-sided I could have taken on half a dozen kids at once. But the boys were happy, and that made me happy too. All part of my new responsibilities, I reckoned, and no actual work involved.

'Telling you, Jen, you're bonkers!' Boy One shouted out in the middle of the game, laughing all the while.

'Yeah, bonkers!' Boy Two giggled. 'And I think I've peed my pants!'

I was delighted. I mean, what more could I have wished for? Confirmation of my new nickname *and* being told I'd made a young human laugh so much he'd wet himself. And I repeat – no work involved. Perfect.

All the same, the Boss didn't seem so impressed when he came into the yard while the contest was still in progress. He gave the boys a right dressing down for risking my teeth with such a stupid carry-on, and the telling-off he gave me was just as stern. But anyway, he ended the lecture by calling me by my nickname as well, so I suspect he wasn't really as annoyed with me as he'd made out. Whatever, I have to give him credit where it's due for warning about the effect the game could have on my teeth.

Ever the one to go out of my way to raise a smile – or even better, a laugh – I adapted the catch-a-stone skill as a solo effort after he'd banned the competitive version. If visitors I recognised came into the yard, I would entertain them by grabbing a pebble in my mouth, tossing it in the air with a flick of my head, then catching it in my teeth before it hit the ground again. It never failed to have the desired effect, so I'd do it over and over again, feeling particularly chuffed when hearing my nickname used in acknowledgement. I used to bark during the whole routine as well, just like I did when playing football or seeing vehicles off the premises, and that definitely added to the sense of excitement.

This went on for years, and had become an expected welcoming ritual at Cuddy Neuk until I hadn't enough front teeth left to let me continue picking up stones. Well, when I say this, what I actually mean is that I *do* still have enough teeth left, but they're so chipped and rotten that the reward just doesn't justify the pain any more. And it hasn't done for a long time now. It just so happens, however, that another favourite tactic I used for amusing the boys back in the day also involved pebbles; or gravel, to be absolutely accurate. But I'm pleased to say it didn't involve my teeth. Quite the opposite, in fact…

LIKE MANY GOOD ideas, this one came about purely by accident. I had just completed one of my daily visits through the gap in the hedge and had gatecrashed a game of football the boys were having at the side of the house, when I had this uncomfortable feeling in the *bahookie*, which is the Scottish word for 'backside', in case you don't know. I'm sure humans must also be familiar with this feeling. You know the one I mean: that feeling you occasionally get in the bahookie region when you've done the type of 'business' I'd just done on the other side of the hedge. Then you suddenly become aware that, in defiance of all your best efforts, a trace of something unwanted has managed to retain its hold on the nether regions of your person, so to speak. It's a perfectly natural occurrence: one I've witnessed being experienced countless times by sheep, cattle and hens, for example – as well as dogs, of course. But the only one of those creatures that has a workable answer to the problem is the dog. That said, I confess to having no knowledge of how humans cope, but I presume their 'superior intelligence' will have provided an adequate solution. I doubt, however, that it could be more effective or eco-friendly than mine.

Yet, when seeing my demonstration of the technique for the first time, the boys dissolved into fits of hysterical laughter. As I say, the realisation that I had a problem in the bahookie region struck me during a game of football, which I was dominating as usual, much to the boys' frustration. When I suddenly stopped dribbling and forfeited my possession of the ball, I'm sure they must have thought that, for once, they'd somehow got the better of me. Obviously, I was keen to set them straight, so wasted no time in dealing with the interruption.

I sat down, raised my hind feet as far up to my face as they'd go, and with my back arched, head thrust forward and my bahookie firmly in contact with the ground, began to propel myself across the grass with a rapid pedalling motion of my front paws. It probably looked to the uninitiated as if I was scooting about on an invisible skateboard, and I thought *both* boys were going to wet themselves this time. They were almost choking with laughter, each with one hand pointing at me, the other clamped to his crotch.

'Go, Jen!' Boy One yelled. 'Ride 'im, cowboy!'

Little Boy Two was too gripped by a fit of the giggles to even speak, far less shout encouragement.

Well now, I thought, if this was the type of reaction I could expect when performing my simple arse-wiping routine on grass, how much more mirth would it generate if I were to up the ante a bit? So, without checking my forward momentum, I changed course and shot onto the gravel surface of the yard.

Talk about bringing the house down! I'd never heard anything like it. Honestly, you could have heard the boys' laughter as far away as Haddington or somewhere. OK, maybe that is a slight exaggeration, but it had certainly been heard inside the Cuddy Neuk farmhouse, that's for sure.

Lady B came rushing out, concern and confusion writ large on her face. To be perfectly honest, I was actually relieved to see her, because I sensed she was going to put a stop to my performance, and there *is* a limit to the amount of gravel-scraping a dog's arse can endure – even a collie's. She gave the boys a right dressing-down. What in heaven's name had they thought they were doing, egging the poor dog on like that? 'And as for you,' she snapped, turning her attention to me, 'I hope I never see you doing that again. Disgusting behaviour, that's what it is!' She didn't half go off on one. Really wiped the floor with me, if you'll pardon the pun.

The Boss had been spreading straw in the cattle shed and must have wondered what all the commotion was about. He came rushing into the yard with a pitch fork still in his hand, but before he had a chance to ask what was up, both boys offered their version of events in garbled unison. They were making a brave attempt at keeping a straight face, but failing miserably, and their father was only marginally more successful.

'Give Jen a break,' he eventually said to Lady B. 'She's only doing what dog's do when needs must. And if I'm honest, I'd do exactly the same in her place … if I was supple enough.' At that, the hint of a smile that had been tugging at the corner of his mouth quickly graduated into a hesitant grin, then a muted snigger, and finally a full-blown guffaw.

The boys joined in, and I contributed that canine version of a laugh I described earlier.

Even Lady B had no resistance to the infection of jollity now permeating the yard. 'Honestly, you lot are the giddy limit,' she tittered. 'One's as bad as the other.' Chuckling quietly to herself, she came over and gave me her customary tickle under the chin. 'And as for you, young lady, I'll forgive you this time, but just make sure you add bum-cleaning to the list of things you *don*'t do in your own nest. OK?'

I knew this might be easier said than done, as any of you who've experienced the same problem will confirm. When you become aware of it, immediate action is essential. And as the Boss pointed out, I was only doing what was right for me. Which got me thinking again about how humans coped. Then it dawned on me why old Doddie used to go about clawing at the seat of his pants all the time, and it made me wonder if Lady B would have thought his method any less disgusting than mine. I concluded that, even if she did, she'd just have to remember that dogs don't have fingers, and the relevant area of our anatomy is well out of reach of our paws anyway.

*

THE BOSS HAD been spreading straw in the cattle shed in preparation for the beasts being brought down from the hill field for the winter. I assumed that keeping an eye on them during the six months or so they'd be housed would be another of my responsibilities, so I was pleased when the Boss, good as his word, took me up the hill a few days beforehand 'to learn a wee bit about their characters'.

There was no sign of them when we went through the field gate, so the Boss decided to wander over to a small rocky knoll, or *knowe* as it's called in Scotland, and sit down for a minute to catch his breath. That was his excuse anyway, but I picked up a vibe that suggested catching his breath wasn't the real reason. I was right, as ever, though the fact that he wasn't even out of breath had actually made the employment of my extrasensory powers unnecessary on this particular occasion. Similarly, it took me only a second to learn the real reason for his decision, and

I did it with nothing but my eyes. The panorama that unfolded before us was truly breathtaking. Even if this hill was just a pimple compared to those I'd been accustomed to at old Doddie's, the views up there had been limited to other hills, while it seemed you could see the whole world and everything in it from here.

The Boss then appeared to read *my* thoughts. 'Yes, I was only a wee boy the first time I sat on this spot, Jen, and I honestly thought I could see forever from here, no matter which way I looked.' He went on to point out some of the most prominent features of the view, from the coast and hills of Fife away over there on the northern side of the Firth of Forth, westward to the rugged profile of Arthur's Seat looming through a haze of mist over Edinburgh's southern flanks, and on to the faint tracery of the world-famous Forth Bridge, just visible far beyond the silhouette of the city's skyline. And all around us lay a patchwork of fields, woods and winding country roads covering the wide, fertile sweep of East Lothian's coastal plain.

It was obvious that what the Boss was saying was more for his own benefit than mine, as none of the things he mentioned meant anything to me. They were all just sounds, but I enjoyed following his gaze when he talked about them, and it was easy to see that visiting this part of the hill field meant a great deal to him. After sitting in silence for a while, he started to recount his memories of that far-off day when he and his grandfather had ridden slowly and steadily all the way up here on the back of the old man's favourite Clydesdale horse. They had come to check the cattle on that occasion too, and just like today, there had been no sign of them anywhere at first. But they'd soon appeared over the crest of the hill: a bunch of twenty bucking and bellowing young animals thundering towards them at the gallop.

'I was scared I'd be trampled to death, Jen, so I tucked myself in behind my grandfather when they started to get too close for comfort.' The Boss gave a little chuckle. 'But I needn't have worried. You see, the old man – my grandfather, that is – had this magic way with cattle. All he did was stand here flapping his arms up and down like a bird and shouting a string of swear words. They stopped in their tracks as if they'd seen a ghost, and not a couple of feet away from us either.' The Boss shook his head and laughed quietly to himself. 'Aye, magic right enough.' He sat and smiled a wistful smile for a bit, then patted me on the back and said, 'Oh, and in case you're wondering where the present bunch are, just have patience – they'll come and find us soon enough, never fear.'

I didn't have long to wait. It started as a dull rumble, and I felt the ground begin to tremble as the sound grew louder. Then there appeared in line abreast over the crown of the hill a couple of dozen fully-grown cattle, heads down, tails up, charging towards us at full tilt.

The Boss laughed out loud. 'There you are, Jen – if you haven't seen a stampede before, you'll be pleased to know you're seeing one now!'

Pleased? He'd obviously misread my thoughts, so the next one I beamed over to him was that he'd better start waving his arms around and shouting swear words pretty damn quick. I was hoping against hope that if humans were also the product their own selective breading, the most appropriate of his grandfather's genes had been selected for this one. To my dismay, though, the Boss made no attempt to do anything. He just stood there, calm as you like, watching the approaching catastrophe with a silly grin on his face.

I'd never been faced with a dilemma like this before. A gang of sheep bearing down on you in this way would have been easily halted, or at least scattered, by any Border collie worth its salt. So, for want of a better idea, I did what my sheepdog instincts told me to do: I lunged forward, crouching low, and stopped stock-still, giving the oncoming mob the never-known-to-fail Border collie hypno-stare. But there's a first time for everything, and it took but a moment to learn that the time had come for the first failure of this old ploy. Cattle weren't sheep – simple as that. Like I say, your average sheep will either freeze or leg it when confronted by a collie bent on bossing them around, but cattle, if this lot were anything to go by, were made of less submissive stuff. If anything, my appearance in their path seemed to encourage them to redouble their commitment to run us into the ground. Taking a swift glance back at the grin still fixed on the Boss's face, I told myself that the most prudent course of action now would be to ignore my instincts, ditch my reputation, swallow my pride and bolt the course – immediately.

But then the weirdest thing happened: without warning and, as far as I could make out, purely of their own volition, the cattle decided to put the collective brakes on. With forelegs outstretched and hind legs flexed to take the strain, their hooves ploughed furrows in the grass as they came to a slithering halt with the lead beast's nose actually touching mine. I double checked the Boss, but he still wasn't flapping his arms, and instead of shouting swear words continued to smile that silly smile, appearing totally unfazed by having miraculously avoided being turned into a human doormat by several tons of rampaging beef.

How the hell had he pulled that one off?

Meanwhile, the cattle had formed a semi-circle round me, all jostling for a turn at sticking their snotty nostrils in my face; just to get to know me better, I supposed. And frankly, I didn't find it a *totally* unpleasant experience. Firstly, because it was a whole lot better than being trampled into the ground, and secondly, because there was actually something soothing about the smell of their breath – or rather, the whiff of their burping. Whatever, it was pleasingly sweet, in a fermented-grass sort of way. And it was plentiful too, because cattle burp all the time, you know, even when they've been having a bit of a stampede.

I was to learn eventually that this burping thing is linked to their habit of chewing the cud, which in turn has something to do with having four bellies and semi-puking their food back up, if that makes any sense to you. I think it's a bit like rabbits double-digesting their food by eating their own droppings, though slightly less revolting. Anyway, the smell of cattle, whatever its source, was to become another feature of my life from then on, as were their inquisitive ways, snotty noses and all.

But such matters were far from my mind that day on the hill field. I was still busy returning my new charges' exploratory sniffs when the Boss called me and beckoned me over to the edge of the knowe. He indicated the sheer thirty-foot drop that fell away just a couple of paces beyond where we'd been sitting, which was something my preoccupation with the more distant views had prevented me from noticing before.

'Let this be a lesson,' he told me. 'Cattle may be a bit flighty at times – unpredictable, even – but they aren't as dumb as some people like to think.' He nodded towards the clifftop we were standing beside. 'And they're certainly *not* suicidal maniacs!'

He burst out laughing like a drain, clearly delighted that he'd succeeded in putting one over on a dog. Congratulations! I mean, he must have been *really* proud of himself. But what did I care? Looking on the positive side, at least I'd learned another thing about the human sense of humour: that it can be pretty damned warped at times. I'd been the victim of what they call a practical *joke*, of all things! In any case, when I thought about it a bit more, I reckoned the Boss had no reason to be in any way cocky about pulling that prank on me, because the person having the last laugh would have been his late grandfather…

Stop a cattle stampede by pretending to be a bird shouting swear words? Aye, pull the other one. But anyway, at least the old boy had managed to put one over on another *human* – even if he was only a kid at the time!

* * * * *

– SEVEN –

PERHAPS I WAS being too self-critical again – and I confess that if I have a fault at all it's probably that I do tend to be too self-critical at times – but after my first few weeks at Cuddy Neuk, I decided to take stock of how my relationship with Lady B had been progressing. After all, she was the one who'd selected me for my current position, so it was important that I should do all I could to justify her faith in me. Although our differences in respect of certain standards and values had been amicably accommodated (at least as far as I was concerned), I still worried slightly about her obsession with cleanliness – or rather what she *thought* of as cleanliness, and with particular regard to smells. It reminded me of the bee old Doddie had in his bonnet about his dogs 'working' sheep, and that bothered me. No, actually, that's not strictly true. To be absolutely frank, it was really her threat to give me a bath that was preying on my mind, so I resolved to get to grips with her way of thinking once and for all.

As luck would have it, this happened to coincide with one of the trips away from home the Boss would occasionally make in connection with a separate activity of his that helped augment the income from Cuddy Neuk's limited acreage. Something to do with 'music', he said it was. Of course, 'music' was just another strange word to me back then, but I was to find out in the fullness of time that, not unlike attitudes towards cleanliness, what pleases the human can sometimes be a source of real irritation to a dog. On second thoughts, that's putting it too mildly, because it's no exaggeration to say that 'torture' would be more appropriate than 'irritation' in the case of what the Boss called music. But that's a side track I'd best not go down just yet. So, as I was about to tell you...

LADY B AND I were alone in the house one day, with the boys at school and the Boss away on one of his 'business' trips. She was busy doing her usual cooking and washing chores in the kitchen, so I decided to do a bit of sniffing around the rest of the house, just to see if I could get to the bottom of something that had been puzzling me since my first night at Cuddy Neuk. It had to do with that refreshing breath of the sea I noticed out in the yard whenever the wind was in the right direction. For some strange reason, there was always a hint of sea air inside the house as well, even when all the doors and windows were closed on a chilly day like the one I'm talking about. It intrigued me. And as memories of being raised at old Doddie's place were still fresh in my mind, I couldn't help but compare the defining 'scents' of both houses.

I should mention first that venturing inside Doddie's home wasn't something his dogs were encouraged to do. In fact, if you were ever caught with even one paw over the threshold, you'd be threatened with the toe of a hobnail boot 'right up yer jacksie'. Not, mind you, that he ever carried out his threats. Old Doddie, like all the livestock farmers I've come across since, always tried to treat his animals with suitable respect, no matter how much they were cursed, bawled at and poked in the ribs when deemed to deserve it. In other words, if those humans were dogs, you'd say their bark was worse than their bite. Usually.

Doddie was sitting on an empty oil drum outside his back door, struggling to cut his toenails with a pair of sheep shears, when I slipped past unnoticed and paid my one and only visit to his kitchen. I was in there for just a moment or two, and didn't dare go very far beyond the doorway. However, even if led blindfold into that place again, and no matter how many years later, I would still have no trouble recognising where I was, so distinctively did it reek of stale pipe smoke, sheep dip and old man's farts. Honestly, I think the ramshackle, mouse-infested doghouse I'd been reared in had a more attractive smell. But, in fairness to old Doddie, I suppose it all depends on what you're used to.

And the same goes for the house here at Cuddy Neuk. My nose being the super-sensitive organ it is, the answer to my puzzlement was quickly revealed on my secret recce that day. There, tucked behind the telly in a corner of the living room was a little green bottle, with a wad of something sticking out the top. I gave this wick thing a good, close-up sniff, just to be absolutely certain, and sure enough, the smell of the sea rising from it was so strong you could have floated a boat on it. Trouble was, it wasn't the *real* smell of the sea, but some sort of phoney chemical imitation. I immediately thought of Lady B's fake-flowery perfume.

Humans! They never fail to amaze me, going to the expense of polluting themselves and their homes with smells that are only poor copies of what nature provides for nothing. What I mean is, if you want the inside of your house to smell like the air outside, just open the bloody doors and windows, for Christ's sake! Same applies to Lady B. Go and have a roll in a patch of wild garlic sometime. Not only will you smell better, but you'll stop being plagued by those damned midgies you complain about every summer as well. Simple.

But that was a long time ago, and although I was still young and relatively inexperienced in the art of dealing with humans, I was smart enough to realise that you do *not* bite the hand that feeds you, either figuratively or literally. I decided to accept Lady B's idea of cleanliness without further deliberation. After all, it really didn't present me with any great hardship, and if I'm honest, there was bugger all I could have done about it anyway. What I had to keep in mind, though, was that Lady B was only doing what was right for her, just as I did, for example, when the urge came upon me to scoot about the yard on my bahookie. Yes, this was one of those subjects on which it would be best if we agreed to differ, which would certainly be how *I* would look on things. Besides, such minor differences aside, Lady B loved me to bits. I knew that because she'd told me, and I confess to the feeling being entirely mutual.

So, with positivity to the fore, I promptly banished all thoughts about cleanliness from my mind … except, of course, that nagging one about the threatened bath.

*

FROM THE VERY first time the Boss was away, I could sense that Lady B missed having him around at night, particularly after the boys had gone to bed and it was just her and me in the living room. She was nervous, being a woman alone with two kids way out in the sticks. I understood that, because I can get a bit jittery myself when it's dark outside and everything is still. That's when the slightest sound can make you open an eye and cock an ear, even if you've been enjoying a quiet snooze. But while I sympathised with how Lady B felt, I reckoned she should have taken comfort from the fact that *I* was there. And truth to tell, I would have felt somewhat peeved if she hadn't, considering the reason she availed herself of my services in the first place was 'to keep an eye on things', as she said to old Doddie – or as he put it, 'to be a kind o' watchdog'. And I knew within myself that she had the most alert set of ears, eyes and nostrils in the watchdog business right there in the living room beside her. Still, to be fair, I hadn't yet had an opportunity to demonstrate those particular qualities, so I resolved to make every effort to maintain as calm an atmosphere as possible until such time as they might be required.

Oh, and the other thing I made sure of maintaining was a respectable distance between myself and the fireplace. Lady B's comments back on my first night about the detrimental effect the heat from the fire had on my natural 'scent' had been quite barbed, and the wounds still stung. It's also worth reminding you that I much preferred to take my nightly rest in a fairly cool spot anyway, so choosing to lie down behind the couch presented no great hardship either. But more to the current point is a fact about watchdogs of which most, if not all, humans may well be unaware: it's that dogs were programmed by Mother Nature back in the wolf era to respond fearlessly and aggressively to the slightest sign of potential danger. Unless bred out of us, coiled springs with teeth is what we are to this day. Yet, in common with many of my canine contemporaries, I admit to not being entirely conscious of this myself, until taking my first stab at watchdogging, that is…

'WILL YOU SETTLE *DOWN*, Jen! There's nothing *there*, so *SHUT UP*! Honestly, you're giving me the bloody creeps!'

I'm afraid this was typical of the reaction I got from Lady B every time I sounded the alarm. And the best of it was that I'd only been growling slightly, not going into the full all-barking, scraping-at-the-door, teeth-bared, let-me-at-'em routine. OK, I appreciate that her inferior sense of hearing prevented her from picking up the minute warning signs I was getting, but why have a watchdog if you persist in ignoring it when it's actually doing its job?

Which is more or less what the Boss told her every time she gave him a report of noteworthy events that had occurred in his absence. 'Jen's only doing what comes naturally,' he'd say. 'You know – guarding the place, protecting you, by her way of it.'

'From behind the *couch*? A fat lot of good that would do, I must say, if an intruder suddenly appeared through the door!'

Well, as you can imagine, Lady B really hurt me with that one. And after all the compromises I'd made to accommodate her odd attitude towards cleanliness and everything. Didn't she realise I was acting in the way the wolf blood in my veins compelled me to do –concealing my presence until the vital moment – employing the surprise element of attack that's the mark of the true hunter? No, clearly she didn't. Which is a perfect example of what I've just been saying about some humans being totally ignorant of the finer points of a guard dog. But anyway, I wasn't going to permit this to make me abandon my resolve to let Lady B have her way when such differences in our outlooks cropped up. As was her wont, she was only doing her best.

I was realistic enough to suspect, however, that my giving her 'the bloody creeps', as she put it, might not enhance my prospects of continuing to sleep in the house when the Boss was away. I instinctively knew as well that the touchy matter of how my presence affected the atmosphere in a warm room hadn't gone away, despite my best efforts to mitigate. As it transpired, though, something totally unforeseen was to become the deciding factor in that respect.

*

ALTHOUGH I'M AS pure-bred as pure-bred can be – an aristocrat of the dog world, you might say – my tastes in food are surprisingly simple. Oh yes, I've seen the rubbish some dogs are plied with in the way of so-called 'treats'. You know, tiny little biscuit things they claim contain cheese or chicken or even exotic ingredients like peacock's giblets or something. Worse still are 'doggie' chocolate buttons. *Choc*olate? Who are they trying to kid? I mean, humans should know that chocolate can poison a dog. Fair enough, there's about as much chocolate in the pet shop variety of chocolate buttons as there is mongrel blood in me, but that's beside the point. What I'm saying is, why call something chocolate while actually stating on the packet that it isn't chocolate at all? It can't be for the benefit of dogs, because dogs can't even read, so presumably it's aimed at the humans who know real chocolate might kill their pet. Crazy! Not that it matters all that much, because most of these treats are made from dried fish guts anyway.

I realise you're probably wondering how I know all this stuff. Same as how I know about all the other stuff I've drawn your attention to: by seeing it on the telly, that's how. Or rather by listening to the Boss when he's shouting at the telly, and I've picked up *all* my general knowledge stuff that way, if you must know.

But as I say, I have very simple tastes in food: my usual dog meal serves me well and I like its natural, unfussy taste. Also, I'm not like those dogs that are always on the lookout for treats, which brings me back to the observation I made a wee while ago about dogs doing tricks. You may recall that my impromptu leap with simultaneous back flip into the Boss's arms was initially described (wrongly) by him as a 'trick', and interpreted (in error) by Lady B as a sign of subservience. Well, I've since seen quite a few examples of pre-conceived tricks some dogs are trained to do to amuse humans, with a measly treat given as a reward for making themselves look 'cute'. There's the simple giving-a-paw trick, the sitting-up-begging trick, the rolling-over-dead one, the standing-on-your-back-legs-and-twirling-like-a-ballerina one and, believe it or not, the balancing-on-your-front-paws-and-peeing-in-the-air speciality for male dogs with exhibitionist tendencies. OK, I think it goes without saying that you've learned enough about my character and self-esteem to realise none of that demeaning nonsense is for me.

Mind you, that's not to say I haven't taken an occasional titbit from a human at meal times, but only, I must stress, by way of helping the human out of a tight corner. I'm talking mainly about junior humans here, and the Cuddy Neuk boys in particular. They'd be in the habit of slipping me a morsel from the dinner table when their parents weren't looking – always morsels of something they didn't like themselves, naturally. But ever a dog to oblige, I'd stealthily gulp the morsel down, even if I didn't *really* like what was on offer. There was, however, a limit to my sense of duty, and I firmly drew the line at Brussels sprouts. In any event, there was never the remotest chance of any party tricks being part of the deal.

I'm sure you're now keen to know what all this has to do with the slight problems that had arisen in connection with my duties as a watch dog and, consequently, the prospects of my being allowed to continue sleeping in the house. Titbits are the clue…

*

IT ALL BEGAN on another of those days when the Boss was away. I was lying on the kitchen floor, watching Lady B preparing food on the worktop: stew, she said it was, made with a nice piece of lean beef and plenty of fresh vegetables. As I mentioned before, I have very simple tastes in food, but I have to admit the smell of that beef really made my mouth water. And Lady B knew it.

'Hmm, I bet you'd like to get your chompers into a lump of this, wouldn't you, Jen. Well, sorry, but it's too expensive, so don't get any daft ideas.'

Of course, she knew me well enough to realise I wouldn't sneak up and snatch a piece off the chopping board when she wasn't looking. I'm not saying I wasn't tempted, mind, but I'm nothing if not a creature of great self control, so resisting the urge posed no problem. Then yet another of those unexpected things happened. Just as Lady B was scooping the meat into her stew pot, she misjudged slightly and a couple of large chunks fell onto the floor. She shot me a cautionary glance, but I didn't move a muscle. In fact, I made a point of feigning no interest by busying myself with a detailed inspection of my front paws.

I could tell by the way Lady B gave a little smirk

that she was suitably impressed. 'Good *girl*, Jen!' she said, scraping the meat onto a little plate. 'You're nothing if not a creature of great self control, I must say. Hmm, most dogs would have made this disappear down their cake hole before it even hit the floor.'

I remained nonchalance personified, my eyes focused now on a dew claw I'd singled out for particular scrutiny.

'And just for being such a good girl, Jen, I'm going to give you a special treat.' With that, Lady B took the plate over to the sink where she gave the chunks of meat a good rinse under the tap. 'It's not fit for human consumption now anyway,' I heard her mumble.

Far from being offended by that remark, I thanked my lucky stars that Lady B's obsession with cleanliness had finally worked in my favour. Little did she know that, even if it had been salvaged from the dung midden, I'd have gobbled up this particular titbit with undisguised relish And considering I'd never tasted raw meat before, this shows that my wolf-rooted instincts were still lurking just below my outward image of successful domestication. I duly wolfed down the chunks of meat.

Lady B watched me do it, shook her head with a little smile and said, 'Glad you enjoyed that, Jen. But don't think we'll be making a habit of it, because we won't. OK?'

She had a way of bringing you down when you were feeling up, that's for sure, but it only served as confirmation that this was how being loved to bits by a human actually worked. I could live with that all right, although I reckoned she might have left me

with even a *faint* hope of tasting raw meat again –
some day.

Still, I went to sleep that night feeling good inside,
telling myself that Lady B might have decided not to
give me that treat at all. Her obsession with cleanliness
had done me a favour, and who was to say the same
stroke of good luck mightn't come my way again –
some day? Luck, however, works in mysterious ways,
and not all of them good, as I was about to discover.
The thing is, no matter how convinced I was in my
mind that wolf blood still ran strong in my veins, my
digestive system was determined to persuade me that
it remained singularly *un*convinced.

I woke up just as dawn was breaking and puked
up the chunks of raw beef right there on my doormat
bed. This didn't present me with any great problem,
of course, because I simply cleaned up the result in
the usual canine manner, being very careful to chew
the stuff slowly and thoroughly this time round. I lay
down again and closed my eyes, ready to snatch a
bit more sleep before the humans of the family came
crashing in to start their day. Then the dreaded shivers
hit me. You know the ones I mean: the shivers that
give you advance notice – usually extremely short –
that any digested material that has been making its
way though your internal workings is now heading
for the exit. At speed.

Talk about a dilemma! The back door I was lying
behind was locked, and the only way I could summon
someone to open it for me was to bark. But if I barked,
Lady B would freak out again, thinking I was warning
her of impending danger – an intruder or a burglar

or a murderer or whatever she called them. I mean, she'd made a big enough fuss about me growling a wee bit, so imagine the state she'd get herself into if I actually *barked*! No, barking was a definite no-no. But so was deciding to stand there doing nothing. My 'business', as Lady B chose to describe it, had to be done ... and with utmost haste.

But cometh such a dilemma for a collie, cometh Mother Nature with a solution – in this case a completely involuntary one as far as I was concerned. Although my mind may have bridged the ages between the present day and the era of my wolfish ancestors, the performance of my guts when it came to processing raw meat was clearly lagging quite a distance behind.

'What the hell is that damn smell?'

As I said before, Lady B didn't swear all that often, but when she did, it was always because she had been driven to it, or so she always claimed. On this occasion, however, the smell she was referring to was only a precursor to the real driving force.

'Oh, *NO-O-O-O*!' she warbled. 'I've gone and stepped *right* in it!'

I stood a respectful distance away, feeling genuinely sorry for Lady B (after all, what had happened wasn't pleasant for her, particularly in her bare feet), but also telling myself it wasn't really my fault. Let's face it, if it hadn't been for Lady B giving me food she considered unfit for human consumption, I wouldn't have been faced with the resultant to-bark-or-not-to-bark dilemma. And even in this moment of personal anguish, my overriding priority had been to protect *her* peace of mind.

Lady B didn't say a word. There wasn't even the slightest hint of reproach in her manner as she opened the back door and ushered me out. To be fair, she certainly was *not* pointing the finger. I'll give her that. What she did do, though, was to wait until she'd seen the boys off to school, then she went and got the Boss's tractor and hauled a little old hen house into a corner of the yard from where it had been sitting forgotten and forlorn at the back of the cattle shed. Still without speaking, she gave it a thorough cleaning out, sprayed it with disinfectant, then brought the old sheepskin rug from the kitchen and laid it on the floor with my water bowl.

'There,' she finally said, gesturing towards the little shack with a welcoming sweep of her hand, 'your very own wee house, Jen. Nice and cosy and comfy and clean. I think you'll be a lot happier in there, won't you, pet?'

All things considered, I had to confess that she was absolutely right. I'd had a taste of living in a human home, and I won't deny I'd enjoyed it – mainly – but at heart I was still as much a nature girl as ever, and independent with it. So, yes, I would indeed be happier in my own wee house, and was thankful to Lady B for providing it. There was, however, just one fly in the ointment (to borrow yet another of your weird human sayings), and that was the inclusion of the old sheepskin rug. I meant no offence to Lay B, because she was only trying her best as usual, but as soon as her back was turned, I back-heeled that woolly old mat right out the door. Lady B was a sensitive soul and would appreciate, I was sure, that a dog's house, no less than a human's, is its castle.

As I settled down for my first night in the old hen house, I do admit there were a few moments when I thought of my humans sitting together across the yard, and I felt a twinge of loneliness, of missing their companionship. But then I thought of the benefits of my solo situation: of having no-one teeter on the verge of a nervous breakdown if I as much as bared my teeth at the sound of a mouse passing wind; of having a nice firm bed of bare floorboards to sleep on; and of having refreshing wafts of night air caressing me through the knot holes in the planks. But most welcome of all was the realisation that no longer would I be under constant threat of a fate worse than death for a dignified nature girl like me. I'm talking, of course, about a bath.

Yes, luck does indeed work in mysterious ways, for who would have thought that *actually* shitting in my own nest for the first time would have earned me such a welcome reward?

* * * * *

– *EIGHT* –

BY THE TIME the Boss came back a couple of days later I was nicely settled into my new quarters and enjoying my daily routine all the more as well. It was November as I recall, and the cattle were all snugly housed for the winter, so keeping an eye on them was a piece of cake. Oops! There I go dipping into that bottomless pit of silly human expressions again. I can't help it, having heard so many in my time. Back in the early days, I could never fathom *any* of them out, but over the years I've gradually managed to make some sort of sense of most. But if I'm absolutely honest, there are still a few that beat me completely. OK, I admit it's just a fluke that 'a piece of cake' was used in a statement about cattle, because I'm sure even the most un-countrified townies among you will know that there *is* actually such a thing as 'cattle cake'. And I can tell you in passing, if you're interested, that I've tasted it and it's about as mouth-watering as that hay I told you about, but with an added squirt of engine oil or something. *Blech*!

Usually, though, there's never even such a flimsy

connection as that between the saying and what's being talked about. Take, for instance, a couple I borrowed earlier: 'No skin off my nose' and 'Cutting off my nose to spite my face.' I mean, in the first example I was talking about Lady B cleaning up a vomit I'd already cleaned up, and in the other I was thinking twice about taking the hump at being called 'subservient' for doing a flying back flip. Is there a link to anyone's nose in either? No. And don't get me started about 'Being as green as you're cabbage-looking', or that other one, 'Twisting somebody round your little finger'. What the hell's all that about?

Humans! They never fail to bamboozle me with their silly sayings.

On the subject of your little finger, though, I'm reminded of a thought I've pondered during many a quiet moment of late: what if dogs had fingers? Intriguing, eh? It was an old Labrador called Sam that first got me toying with the prospect. See, you may think us farm dogs are a bit cut off from what's going on in the wider world, not being in regular contact with other dogs and all that. Well, nothing could be further from the truth; not in my case anyway. I mean, I've been to boarding kennels a couple of times, and the humans who visit us here at Cuddy Neuk often have dogs with them too, so I'm as worldly wise as I need to be. I certainly am, so don't you worry about that.

Anyhow, this old Lab called Sam used to come here with his human, a little female one who dropped by occasionally to 'do' Lady B's hair, whatever that meant. Something to do with making it look different,

I think, but it always looked much the same to me when they eventually emerged from the house. It just didn't blow in the wind as freely and had a smell that irritated my nose, although it didn't seem to bother old Sam. Sam, by the way, was the laziest dog you ever met. Honest, if you knew him, you'd say the same. All he ever wanted to do was eat, then lie about sleeping and passing wind. Those stealth farts of old Sam's were really soft, silent ones – almost inaudible, even to me. Came out wearing slippers, was what the Boss said about them. But wow, did they hum! I liked old Sam, though – I truly did – and it was him that got me thinking seriously about what it would be like if dogs had fingers – and thumbs too, of course.

It's not as if Sam thought about things all that much him*self*, mark you. No, there were times I used to sit for ages watching him lying here in the yard, with his face on his paws and his eyes only half open and everything, and I used to reckon he was deep in thought. But he wasn't – he was just lying there with nothing going on 'between the lugs', as old Doddie would have put it. Ages could go by without me being able to pick up one single thought wave from Sam, and you already know how sharp I am at picking up thought waves. Then, all of a sudden, this idea would pop into Sam's head and I'd latch onto it right away. Usually the idea didn't amount to much, though – usually only some ploy he'd dreamed up to wheedle an extra titbit or two from his human, then back to sweet, idle oblivion.

But this one time he started thinking about his hobby (which I hadn't known about before, by the way), and this hobby of his was collecting stones. Just ordinary stones, like the ones I used to fling in the air and catch in my mouth in the days before my teeth got too knocked about, but slightly bigger stones than that. Stones about the size of tennis balls were what Sam collected. He used to snorkel for them, apparently – submerging his head in the water of a wee burn that ran through the woods where he went on walks with his little human. Her that 'did' Lady B's hair. Anyway, he'd carry the latest stone he'd *dooked* for all the way home, where he'd lay it carefully in a long line of similar sized stones he'd already collected. How weird is *that*? But if you think that's weird, just wait till you hear what he did next. He started making the stones into *patterns*. That's right – plain circles first, then circles with tails on them, like one of those shapes humans make with a pen or something when they're writing their words down on paper. Words like the ones helping you read my thoughts in that book of yours right now. Imagine a lazy old Lab thinking of that. Weird isn't in it! Mind you, Sam didn't get any further than that one shape – the letter 'Q' he was told it was called – but it was weird enough to get me thinking seriously about what dogs could do if we had fingers.

We'd be able to write for a start. And draw pictures too, if we wanted to, although we probably wouldn't bother, because we'd already have developed that camera contraption that makes pictures without any buggering about with pencils and stuff. That's the thing about dogs with fingers, we'd only make things that helped us have more time for fun. Well, I would anyway, and even those idiot brothers of mine would as well, just as soon as we'd domesticated our humans to do all the work for us. And we wouldn't bother with all that selective breeding rigmarole when it came to our humans either. No way. All we'd do is make sure they held onto that work ethic thing they've tried to instil into us dogs for so long. Give them a taste of their own medicine, is the expression you'd probably use yourselves. Damn right we would.

OK, so some of you may be asking what we'd do about driving cars and building houses and growing crops and all that other stuff humans regard as essential. Well, the simple answer is that none of these things are essential to dogs anyway, and even if we did need them occasionally, we'd simply train our humans to do them for us. Oh, and it just struck me: what would there be to stop the likes of old Sam from being in charge of building houses, for example? With his experience of putting stones together, all he'd need to do with his new fingers would be to draw up some plans for his humans and the rest would be – yes, you've guessed it – a piece of cake.

Same would go for medicine and music and telly programmes. With fingers and thumbs there's nothing dogs couldn't do as well as humans. I mean, it's all down to intelligence, isn't it? Yes, and if creatures of the same species as old Doddie can paint barn doors and make five-bar gates and play bagpipes, there would be nothing to stop a creature of superior intelligence (like me, for instance) from doing the same – if not better. Mind you, I'd give bagpipes a miss, and I'll tell you why later … if I remember.

So, give those ideas some thought sometime. Then think about how you humans would have got on if you'd started out with paws instead of hands. Hmm, see what I mean? You wouldn't have become the so-called master species then, would you? And do you think dogs would be daft enough to walk around picking up *your* turds? Dream on!

But anyway, such notions were still years away from entering my mind when I welcomed the Boss back home a couple of days after I'd been relieved of my duties as a live-in guard dog. The moment his car door opened, I started my slow creep forward, smiling the smile I knew beguiled him, then launched myself into a perfectly executed flying back flip. He caught me in his arms as securely as ever, and we looked into each other's eyes while exchanging affectionate thought waves. There's no doubt the vibes I was beaming up at him were more potent than normal, but I wanted to ensure that, when he'd been told why the old hen house had been dragged into the yard, more sympathy than censure would be coming my way.

Right on cue, Lady B appeared in the farmhouse doorway. 'Just keep holding her belly-up like that,' she called out to the Boss as she hurried towards us. 'There's something I want to do.'

'Happy days!' I said to myself. I'd been looking forward to another tummy tickle for a long time, but being treated to one at this particular moment – especially from Lady B herself – was more than I'd dared hope for.

'That's right,' she continued, 'just hold her nice and steady and I'll do the necessary.' At that, she produced a little packet from behind her back and pulled out some wads of white stuff that smelled of disinfectant. 'I'll give her underparts a good going-over with these Dettol wipes – get rid of all that ingrained dirt and any germs that go with it.' She then proceeded to scrub away frantically. 'Yes, you may have escaped having a bath, Jen,' she panted, 'but this is the next best thing.'

Actually, apart from the nose-nipping smell, I quite enjoyed the experience. It wasn't as gentle as the tummy tickle she'd given me before, but I didn't really mind. That's another thing about us collies: we don't mind a bit of rough treatment when it comes to tummy tickles – or in other words being given a good old scratch – particularly when it comes to the parts we can't reach ourselves. It's a pity I had to find out the way I did, though, and I wasn't too keen on what happened next either.

'Just put her down on the ground,' Lady B told the Boss, 'and I'll finish off her beauty treatment there. That's right – hold her by the collar and I'll rub this powder into her coat. Get rid of any livestock lurking in that thick fur.'

'You're not suggesting she's got *fleas* next?' frowned the Boss, looking a bit bemused by the whole performance.

'Can't be too careful,' Lady B breezed. 'Anyway, no bugs will survive a dousing of this stuff. Kills everything from ear mites to cockroaches and scorpions.'

'Might kill the bloody dog as well, if that's the case!'

'Nah. Got it from the vet. Specially formulated for the job, he said. Even smells nice.'

Well, that was entirely a matter of opinion. To me, it smelled too much like that fake-flowery scent Lady B polluted herself with. And combined with the stench of disinfectant from the belly scrub, it was enough to make you throw up. Which I almost did. But, ever the stoical collie, I endured the humiliation without so much as a whimper.

'That's a clever *girl*!' Lady B beamed when it was all over. She ruffled the top of my head. 'You en*joy*ed that, didn't you? Ye-e-e-s, of *course* you did. And just think,' she went on, nodding towards the old hen house, '– a nice wee house of your very own, all nice and clean and disinfected, just like you are yourself now, eh? Bet you can't wait till bedtime.'

The Boss said nothing, but gave me one of his knowing winks.

I WAITED UNTIL the humans had gone indoors, then headed straight for the dung midden.

Second only to a roll in wild garlic, a roll in a midden is just what you need to restore nature's fragrance to a fur coat defiled by chemicals. Mind you, I'm not talking about rolling about in the more *mature* material that's in the centre of a midden – you know, the stuff that steams and reeks to high heaven when you're filling your dung spreader on a frosty morning. No, no, that would be a wee bit *too* robust. No, what I'm talking about is rolling about in the stuff on the perimeter of the midden, the stuff that's mainly mouldy old straw, laced with just a smattering of semi-dried 'deposits'. It provides the desired effect without dulling the lustre of your coat. Honestly, five minutes wallowing in that stuff will provide enough of an antidote to the stench of disinfectant and insecticide to make not only your fur smell right again, but after just one night, the interior of your own wee house as well. Oh, aye – the subtle aromas of the farm. Not to be sniffed at, if you see what I mean.

I suppose it shouldn't have come as much of a surprise that Lady B didn't see eye to eye with me on that one. It was only a few hours after I'd taken my midden bath that I bumped into her and the Boss when making my way into the yard following a stint of overseeing duties in the cattle shed. As I touched on earlier, there wasn't much to do in that respect, being winter. If the cattle weren't munching away at the hay in their racks, they'd be munching away at chopped Swedish turnips in their troughs. And if they weren't doing that, they'd be lying in their straw, chewing the cud, which is that disgusting habit of re-eating half-digested food I described to you a while back.

Frankly, supervising cattle in winter can get a bit boring for an all-action collie like me. Can't even entice them into chasing me, which some of them like to do out in the fields in summertime. And that can be good fun – sort of like what humans call 'playing chicken'. You know, letting them charge right up to you before nipping through a hedge or under a fence or something at the last second. I got the idea from that practical joke the Boss played on me the first time he took me up the hill field. I'm pretty sure I told you about that, but even if I didn't, you get the picture anyway. It was a battle of nerves and agility: a battle I always won, naturally.

But, no, there wasn't any chance of playing such games in winter, so I just used to lie in the feed passage that runs up the middle of the shed dividing one cattle 'court' from the other. The hay racks and feed troughs extend the length of it, so there were usually plenty of noses sticking through that I could go and sniff, if I wanted to. As you know, I quite like the smell of their breath – the cattle's that is – particularly that fresh, grassy smell you get when they're out grazing. No offence to the beasts – because I really quite like them, whatever they're eating – but the burped whiff of regurgitated Swedes really doesn't have the same appeal. So, I didn't go and sniff their noses all that much. What I did, if I got too bored, was slip under the troughs that line either side of the feed passage and then creep around the courts, imagining we were out on the hill field or somewhere and I was patrolling the herd, making sure none of them did anything stupid, like starting a stampede or something again. Trouble was, in the shed, the beasts were only interested in lying there chewing the cud and didn't pay me any heed at all.

That sort of behaviour could be a bit demoralising for a dog that didn't think too deeply about things, but I knew full well that the cattle were only acting in such a peaceful and contented way because they felt safe in the knowledge that I was there looking after them. Also, if I ever felt *really* fed up, I could always go and supervise the hens scratching about in their run for a change.

The only real risk you encounter while moving about among housed cattle, apart from maybe being kicked in the face if you sneak up behind them when they're feeding, is the chance of standing in one of their 'pats', which they deposit at random in their straw bedding. Come spring, that's what middens are made from, in case you don't know. But there's also the possibility of having hidden portions of 'pat' stick to your rear end when you take a seat in the straw. And this is what triggered that outburst of Lady B's that I mentioned at the start of this trip down memory lane. You probably remember the one I'm talking about: the one when she called me *mingin*' and told the Boss never to let me into the house again?

'She's *mingin*'!' she said. 'Just look at those dangleberries clinging to her rear end!'

Remember the outburst now? Well, *I* do, even if *you* don't, and I'm never likely to forget the injustice of it. The point is, dangleberries, or whatever you call them where you come from, are what folk hereabouts call those little pellet-type balls that stick to your fur after you've done your 'business' and haven't scooted about thoroughly enough on your bahookie afterwards. As I said before, I don't know what humans do to remedy the problem, but if they do it by skidding around on their arses as well, I suspect they do it on the floor of the bathroom, judging by the pong wafting out after they've been in there a while. Oh, and the sly spraying of fake sea air before you come out is never likely to fool the family dog, by the way.

But that's your affair, and it's neither here nor there in the current context. For what we're dealing with here is a total misapprehension of the facts by Lady B, and the consequent sullying of my reputation in terms of personal hygiene. That's what got me going about Lady B's fixation with cleanliness in the first place: why I didn't entirely agree with it, I mean.

It hadn't occurred to her that those dangleberries (if they weren't in fact just sticky willies as the Boss suggested) might have been an indirect result of my supervisory duties in the cattle shed, rather than any neglect of personal hygiene. That said, now that I think about it, I should have remembered that Lady B doesn't have the super-sensitive nose of a dog, so couldn't have sniffed the difference between cattle-sourced and dog-sourced dangleberries even if she'd tried. Also, thinking back, she hadn't yet witnessed my bahookie-wiping routine as performed for the boys after that game of football I told you about. So, OK, fair enough, I was probably being a bit hard on her. But no matter, it all worked out fine in the end, because, as you know, I went on to adopt a conciliatory attitude towards Lady B's cleanliness obsession, and I refused to let the matter get in the way of the wonderful relationship that has only grown stronger between us with each passing year.

To illustrate the point: putting that relationship into the hypothetical context of dogs having fingers, if Lady B chanced to be one of the humans in my 'ownership', so to speak, I would have no hesitation in taking her on as my housekeeper.

But reverting to the reality of that day in the yard

when she told the Boss never to allow me into the house again, the Boss's reaction, as you may recall, was just to smile that wee smile of his and give me a wink, which was enough to convince me that my banishment was unlikely to be absolute – as far as he was concerned at any rate.

* * * * *

– NINE –

THE NEXT DAY happened to be one of the days Lady B went off in her car to 'do the shopping', which she was in the habit of doing two or three times a week – at least. I was sitting in the yard when the Boss saw her off, and I watched him amble back inside the house, leaving the door open behind him. He didn't actually *beckon* me to follow, but he did glance back at me briefly before disappearing inside, and if a glance was meant to be as good as an invitation, I reckoned that one had served the purpose well.

All the same, I stepped into the house in an appropriately tentative fashion, taking care to poke my nose into the living room to test the Boss's reaction before venturing further. I was pretty sure my reading of the vibes had been right, but you can never be too careful when it comes to breaking a banishment rule, and the last thing I wanted was to appear in any way presumptuous. After all, it was unlikely the Boss would have wanted to upset Lady B either, and the 'come hither' glance he'd thrown me across the yard may only have been an invitation to meet him at the back door for one of his little chats. I mean the type of chat I told you about that could have caused the casual observer to think he was actually talking to himself. But I should have known better than to doubt my own judgement.

'Come away in, Jen,' he said when he noticed me. 'Come on – in you come – nothing to worry about.'

He was sitting in his favourite seat, with the telly flickering away in the opposite corner of the room. I knew from past experience that he liked to watch the lunchtime TV news, provided he didn't have any urgent work to do about the farm, that is.

'Just you sit here at my feet, lass. That's it. My legs'll shield you from the heat of the fire – no need to lie behind the couch any more.' He smiled at me and tapped the side of his nose. 'And don't you worry, I'll spray the place with Air Wick before Her Ladyship comes back – just in case.'

I was one move ahead of him, though. An hour or so later, while he was still blissfully preoccupied with whatever was on the telly, my super-sensitive hearing warned me that Lady B's car was coming down the road, so I nipped outside and took up my usual visitor-greeting position in the middle of the yard.

'Hello there, Jen,' she grinned as she stepped from the car. 'Nice of you to come and meet me.'

Something about the way she said that told me she was onto me, but undeterred, I gave her my customary welcome: big smile, wiggly body, head dipped deferentially. And the ploy seemed to work. She crouched down, tickled me under the chin and, wonder of wonders, kissed me on the head. Yes, actually *on* my head.

'You really are a one-off,' she chuckled. 'You're the most *sleekit* creature I've ever come across … and I love you to bits.'

Sleekit. Now, here was yet another word I hadn't heard before. But for once, no lengthy process of working out what it meant was required. In a combination of female intuition and an exchange of thought waves between Lady B and myself, I quickly realised she was describing me as sly, underhand and devious, and in this case, disobedient too – but, and it's an extremely important 'but', in the most disarming way as well. An understanding had been forged between two lady bitches, and it's one that has stood the test of time. But I've never abused her trust by overstepping the mark. I've never jumped up on the couch, I've avoided sitting close to the fire and I've always made my exit from the house before she comes back home, while relying, most importantly, on the Boss giving the place a timely blast of Air Wick – just in case.

Anyway, that was the start of my learning lessons 'at the Boss's knee', so to speak. As I've said before, he tended to shout at the telly a lot, and that's how I picked up my general knowledge – mostly. A breed of humans called 'politicians' was what he shouted at more than anything else. 'Bunch of bloody numpties!' he'd shout. 'Two-faced, lying bastards – thieves and parasites!' Things like that. And this never changed much over the years, so I know as much about politicians now as I did at the start, which is next to nothing. To be perfectly frank, I've an idea the same applies to the Boss. And to be perfectly honest, that's why I never liked watching the news all that much, because it always seemed to be about politicians, and the Boss always shouted the same stuff, which means I really didn't learn anything – except swear words, of course.

No, what I liked best were programmes about animals that came on after the news sometimes. The Boss liked them too, so he'd sit about watching them if there was nothing too urgent for him to do about the farm – and even if there was, when the notion took him. 'Looks like rain, Jen,' he'd say. 'Better not start cutting the hay today.' Things like that. What puzzled me was that he'd use the same excuse whether it was hay-making time or not. Humans! They never fail to puzzle me – making lame excuses for watching telly when they should be doing something else.

Anyway, this one time – maybe a couple of years after I commenced my duties here – there was this programme on the telly about a big dog show called Cuffs, or Turfs, or Crisps. Something like that. Anyway, I've always remembered a couple of things about it, even if I can't remember the name. First, there was this sort of running competition for dogs – an obstacle course or steeple chase, I think they called it – and there was only one dog having a go at a time; showing how quickly it could complete the course, if you see what I mean. You should have seen it, this dog that won it, racing up and over ramps and gates, and through lines of zigzag poles, and in and out of tunnels and tubes, then turning fast and jumping more gates and ramps and finally leaping at top speed into its human's arms. It didn't do a flying back flip, I hasten to add, but even so, the crowd of humans watching went wild and the dog won a prize. Oh, and the dog was a Border collie, if you haven't already guessed.

Yes, I was really taken with that event. It was something I knew I would have been really good at, and I did beam strong vibes at the Boss to let him know I thought it would be a great idea if he built a course like that for me, maybe in that patch of grass at the side of the house where the boys played football. But it never happened, so I just had to content myself with playing football with the boys, and catching stones, and biting the front tyres of cars and vans and trucks and everything as they left the farm.

But anyhow, this other thing I really liked about that dog show on the telly was the competition for the best dog. Supreme Champion, I think they called the winner. And to win the prize, all the dogs had to parade about the ring with their humans, walking and trotting and looking really subservient, then stand in a long line being peered at by some big-deal human judge who finally stuck a plastic flower thing on the dog he thought was the best looking and best walker and trotter and stuff like that. 'A collection of shifty bullshit merchants' is what the Boss once called a group of politicians in a similar line-up. But that's neither here nor there, because all I was interested in anyway was this one dog, the one that got the Supreme Champion prize.

You should have seen it! Or rather *him*. A big Afghan Hound called Boris. Talk about handsome!

Noble as well – lordly, even, and suave with it. Honest, I'd never seen anything like it. Now, don't get me wrong – I wasn't any silly wee lassie that gets her knickers in a fankle over some swanky, show-off poser with big hair that cocks his leg with what you're supposed to think is 'style'. No, no, I wasn't that easily impressed, although Boris did cock his leg and pee on the judge's foot, but with just the right measure of panache. I mean, he *did* have class. You couldn't deny it.

Oh yes, that Boris – I *really* fancied him. Don't ask me why, because I don't exactly know, particularly since he was only a picture on the telly and I couldn't even smell him. No, it was just something about the look of him that got me a wee bit … well, ex*cit*ed. Yes, that's all I can say about it, although I'm pretty sure every female human will know what I mean, even if she's already harnessed to a boss man the way Lady B is. And for all I know, maybe even es*pec*ially if she's already harnessed to a boss man the way Lady B is.

But I know what you're thinking: you're thinking I'm just a plain, unsophisticated, wee country bitch that would be hard pushed to attract *any* dog, never mind a Supreme Champion type like Boris the beautiful Afghan. Well, let me tell you, that's where you're wrong. I'd only been here a day at the most when the first suitors came to call, and I wasn't even in heat, or what you'd more politely call 'season'. Not that such a minor detail mattered to the callers in question: predominantly scruffy part-collies from other farms in the vicinity. They were rough-and-ready mutts that would hump anything from a hibernating hedgehog to a scabby rabbit with myxomatosis. All they required of a target for their lust was that it should be breathing and slow off the mark. So, when their noses told them a fresh-as-a-daisy young bitch had entered their patch, their willies promptly pointed the way to where the promise of *real* pleasure awaited.

And don't kid yourselves that just because I was young and inexperienced I didn't know what all that humping business was about. You aren't brought up on a sheep farm without being constantly confronted by such 'acts of nature' – and I don't mind telling you that sheep *dogs* are just as keen on it as the sheep. There are no surprises in that, of course, for when you get down to the nitty-gritty, it's an indisputable fact that without randy animals, dog-breeding shepherds like old Doddie would be out of business.

Anyway, cold-calling suitors have always got short shrift from me. And I mean *all* of them, especially those that made regular six-monthly visits to coincide with what their noses told them would be the most favourable window of opportunity. Don't get me wrong – I'm completely 'straight', as you humans say, and while I could never be described as having an inflated opinion of myself, I do admit to being extremely attractive to the opposite sex. Oh, and if you're thinking that any bitch *would* be when the only dogs sniffing around her were scruffy rakes like the ones I've just described, then I'd respectfully suggest that this reflects more on the quality of male dogs hereabouts than on my personal physical allure. As mentioned before, I'd already witnessed what producing litters of guzzling pups did to my mother's body, and I had no intention of sacrificing the God-given beauty of mine merely to satisfy the desires of some horny old cur that fancied a quick knee-trembler behind the cattle shed. If they were that desperate for sexual gratification, their best idea would be to go fuck them*sel*ves. That was how I looked at it.

Having said all that, the dearth of local suitors of Boris the Afghan Hound's calibre was something I was ultimately obliged to accept, albeit reluctantly. You can't have everything in life – I've learned that too. But I'm pleased to say that my hard-nosed attitude towards no-hope opportunists did pay off. In every case but one, that's to say. While all the others eventually admitted defeat and took their horny habits elsewhere, one persistent individual kept trying his luck...

Shuggie, a shabby collie-cross-mongrel, belonged to the gardener at a big country house near here, and what he lacked in refinement (which was just about everything) he made up for in sheer determination. He was nothing if not dogged. I'll give him that. But if Lady B thought *I* was mingin', it's just as well she never got up close and personal with that walking flea bag. Shuggie, however, was crafty enough never to venture into the yard, contenting himself with skulking about on the perimeter of the steading, watching and waiting for the slightest sign that I might at last be ready to accept his advances. As if! There was about as much chance of that as there was of Boris the Afghan leaping out of the telly and carrying me off into the sunset.

But, credit where it's due, Shuggie did know his place and never *really* pushed his luck. He was just a background presence at Cuddy Neuk: a bit like the sea air, though a sadly putrid incarnation of it. Yet I actually quite liked him, in a commiserating sort of way, and always from a respectable distance. Little would he have realised, poor sod, that while I shunned him every day, I dreamed of Boris every night. Shuggie, you see, was one of life's natural losers, but he bore his misfortune with quiet resignation, and never bothered anyone – as a rule.

*

OF COURSE, WHAT Shuggie and the other mutts were up to was just what came naturally. They were responding to the ancient spur of nature to pass their individual characteristics onto the next generation of their own species (while drawing a veil over the equally strong urge of a few to attempt the creation of totally *new* species, like barking hedgehogs and bone-gnawing rabbits). Nature, like luck, works in mysterious ways.

Which brings me back to that experience I had with the two young lambs at old Doddie's place. You probably remember the incident – the one when he caught me being chased by animals that he thought should have seen *me* as the chaser. Yet we were having fun, the way I've seen many other unlikely playmates do on the telly: lions and antelopes, gorillas and humans, squirrels and cats, mice and mouse-eating spiders, fox cubs and day-old chicks, to name but a few. Mind you, I've often thought the only obvious difference between gorillas and humans is that one is hairier than the other. But you see what I'm getting at: without interference from humans, different creatures coming together in the right conditions will probably get along just fine. Unless something like hunger gets in the way, of course.

And I'm not just talking about what I've seen on the telly. Take, for instance, the case of the two little kittens Lady B came home with one day, to keep the place nice and free of mice, she said. Frankly, I didn't see the need, as the few mice I'd noticed about the place weren't causing any great problem: just nibbling the occasional grain of oats or barley, or even the odd flake of cow cake which, as I've mentioned before, they'd be more than welcome to. And anyway, they were hungry and weren't harming any other creatures in order to survive.

I don't mind admitting that I'm no great fan of cats, but I didn't bear any grudge against that pair, just so long as they didn't try taking over my 'zone', that's all. But don't go imagining that I actually *played* with them. Absolutely not. I mean, it's one thing to tolerate cats, but an entirely different one to actively encourage them, and I've never hesitated to confess that I'm a bit of a traditionalist in that respect. You bet I am.

But anyhow, it's actually cattle I'm singing the praises of here. You see, what happened was this: that pair of kittens managed to clamber their way into one of the hay racks in the cattle shed this particular day. They're very good at clambering up things, cats are. Better than dogs – I won't deny it. So, this pair must have clambered onto the top of the hay in this particular hay rack. It was winter, and the cattle – a bunch of young heifers – had just been given their last feed of the day. I watched them getting stuck in, then went off to my own wee house and settled down for the night, forgetting all about the heifers and their hay. I mean, what was to remember anyway? I'd seen cattle being fed countless times and nothing exciting ever happened, short of catching the whiff of a specially sweet belch if they happened to have been treated to a feed with locust beans in it. Really sweet smelling, locust beans are. I even remember the boys used to pick bits of them out of the cattle troughs and eat them themselves, because they tasted sweet too, they said. I had a nibble myself once, but didn't share their enthusiasm, to be honest. I did like the smell, though – when converted into a burp by a cattle beast, that is.

So, next morning, after I'd watched Lady B letting the hens out (they lived in a hen house near that grassy bit where the boys played football), I nipped round to the cattle shed to see how the heifers were doing. I knew the Boss would be shovelling chopped Swedes into their troughs, so there'd be plenty of barging and butting going on. They're a bit selfish and aggressive when it comes to getting stuck into chopped turnips, most cattle, so I usually joined in the fun by running about behind them barking like fury. I never got near enough to get kicked in the face, though. Too smart for that, although I say so myself.

Well, all of this seemed pretty normal, until I

glanced up at that hay rack I was talking about. I could scarcely believe my eyes, for those hungry heifers had actually left a little clump of hay – a bit like a bird's nest – all neat and undisturbed in one corner of the rack. And guess what was curled up on top of it. That's right, you've guessed – those two little kittens Lady B had come home with. Imagine that! A pen full of hungry heifers, greedy beasts that would normally tug away at hay in a rack until there's wasn't a leaf left, had actually left some of their food untouched to let two little kittens have a cosy kip for the night. I'd never seen anything like it.

But anyway, what I'm saying is that most animals will get along just fine with different kinds of animals when left to their own devices, if you see what I mean. I mean, cattle and kittens for instance – who would have believed it? Oh, and it wasn't because the kittens had peed in the hay or anything like that, if that's what you're thinking. No, no, not at all, for the cattle scoffed the lot just as soon as the kittens had clambered down. And I can tell you without fear of contradiction that cattle will *not* eat hay that cats have pissed on. That's one thing about cattle – they're quite fussy eaters.

But while I'm only too ready to give cattle beasts credit for being kindly towards creatures of a different species, I think you'll agree, modest though I am, that the example I've just given will seem fairly unexceptional when set against a particular one that involved me. Here's what happened...

THE BOSS HAD been having some building work

done – repairs to the old stable where the young bulls were kept, I think it was – and the builders had left a heap of unused sand to be picked up next time they were passing. Months later it was still there. I'd noticed a she rabbit had made a burrow on one side of it in the meantime, and it wasn't hard to guess her purpose. Once you get to know rabbits, you know that when they go to the bother of making a burrow the chances are that a batch of new rabbits is on the way. And sure enough, one evening a few weeks later I noticed two or three of the youngsters peeking out at sunset and taking a few exploratory hops round the entrance to their den. You have to hand it to mother rabbits – they're very cautious creatures when it comes to keeping their youngsters out of sight in daylight. What they're not very good at, though, is predicting when humans like the Boss are likely to come along with a hydraulic bucket on their tractor and demolish the snug little nest that's home sweet home to you and yours. But, fortunately for her, I was one step ahead of the game – again.

It was late morning the following day when I saw the Boss approaching the heap with his tractor, duly mounted with its front-loader bucket and all set to shift the sand to who-knows-where. Now, as you can imagine, even a Border collie with extrasensory communication skills like mine would be hard pushed to convey a warning on behalf of a rabbit family to a human being who's bent, albeit unwittingly, on making them homeless. I did try barking at the bucket as it was driven towards the sand, but the Boss must have mistaken my intended message for some sort of variation on the front-tyre-biting routine I've told you about. Things can get frustratingly complex when humans fail to read the vibes that are being beamed over to them, and although I credit the Boss with being as quick on the uptake as most in this regard, there are occasions when I despair. And this was one of them.

As luck would have it, however, it was almost lunchtime, so the Boss stepped down from his tractor and headed for the farmhouse without disturbing a single grain of sand. But he was still blissfully unaware of the dire consequences that would await his sand heap squatters when the time came to commence work again. And while I wanted to believe that he would rather avoid being responsible for such a callous act, I couldn't envisage what he might or might *not* do to avoid it either. Fast-multiplying, crop-nibbling rabbits aren't, after all, the most welcome visitors to any farmer's land. I preferred not to think about it, but sprang into immediate action instead.

When the Boss returned after lunch, I had just plucked the last baby bunny from the burrow by the scruff of the neck and was setting off at the trot to where I'd already deposited its siblings. I noticed the Boss watching me, scratching his head, the expression on his face suggesting he thought I'd taken leave of my senses. I've no doubt, though, that having thought about it for a moment, he finally decided I was carrying the little critter away to drown in a ditch or something – you know, ridding the farmyard of a piece of vermin, that sort of idea. Which is another example of humans jumping to conclusions about how different creatures react to each other, or are *expected* to by humans.

In this instance, I'd observed that the mother rabbit just about took a fit when I arrived on the scene, no doubt convinced that I regarded her offspring as tasty morsels to be taken away and gobbled up at my leisure. And who could blame her? That was what came naturally to wolves of old, and what many dogs had since been *trained* to do by humans. I saw it on the telly once: how skinny, hound-type dogs had been fooled into chasing a dummy rabbit round a track so that their human masters could make money by guessing which one was the fastest fool. The Boss explained the whole thing to me at the time, but I couldn't really make any sense of it at all.

Anyhow, the mother rabbit needn't have panicked, because I only carried her babies through the hedge where I went to 'do my business', then deposited them on a grassy bank that was a popular hang-out for rabbits. There were burrows everywhere. All she had to do was pick an empty one, set up house and prepare to teach her brood how to eat their own droppings – or whatever tricks of survival rabbits do actually hand down to their young. I knew she'd kept a watchful eye on me from a discreet distance throughout the rescue mission, which had been a somewhat frantic exercise for me. So, not surprisingly, I was now ready for an afternoon nap, and I duly took one, while giving the impression to any nosey human that I was supervising the hens scratching about in their run.

Truly, a collie's 'work' is never done – not if you're a free spirit like I am, and an altruistic one to boot. I mean, can you imagine a cat going to all that bother to save a bunch of baby rabbits from being bulldozed to death? No, I don't think so. Believe it or not, I once saw a cat climb in through a window of the farmhouse with a dead sparrow in its mouth. And would you believe the sparrow was supposed to be a *gift* for the humans? That's what cats will do, you see – they'll stalk a poor wee bird for ages, just so they can kill it and give it away to some humans they're trying to impress. And I suppose they think the humans are going to be delighted to have a dead bird dumped at their feet. Aye, right!

But that's cats for you: sly, underhand and devious – or *sleekit*, to use the word Lady B did to describe my 'secret' indoor visits to watch TV with the Boss. Yet when you really think about it, cats are in a class of their own in that respect. You have to admit it. And when you really, *really* think about it, you'd be forgiven for concluding that Lady B had actually been guilty of a grave insult by using a word to describe *me* that's more suited to a fuckin' cat.

Humans! Honestly, it's just as well I've been blessed with such an accommodating disposition.

* * * * *

– TEN –

HAVE YOU EVER noticed that a dog always looks you straight in the eye when you meet? That's what we do, and we'll even look you in the eye before we bite you on the ankle. And that isn't to lull you into a false sense of security, believe me. No, we'll usually only bite you on the ankle after we've decided you've got it coming, and we decide that by looking you in the eye, the window to your soul, the communication centre, the place where the vibes come from. As I've hinted at before, if we, with the aid of our highly developed gift of extrasensory perception, read something in your eyes that advises us to treat you as a potential threat, or even just a dog-hating misfit, we'll either just growl and curl a lip, or if the vibes are bad enough and we haven't been 'trained' to ignore them, we'll sink our teeth into your ankle before *you*'ve had a chance to have a go at *us*.

Of course, we don't always do the full eye contact thing when meeting other dogs, but we do usually sniff each other's bahookies. You've doubtless seen us doing it and wondered why. Well, here's one explanation the Boss has repeated to me many times over the years…

The dogs they had a party; they came
from near and far.
And some dogs came by aeroplane
and some by motor car.
They went into the venue and signed
the visitors' book,
Then each one hung his arsehole upon
a handy hook.

One dog was not invited, and this aroused his ire.
He rushed into the meeting place and loudly
shouted 'FIRE!'
The dogs were so excited they had no time to look,
So each one grabbed an arsehole from off the
nearest hook.

This is a sad, sad story, for it is very sore
To wear another's arsehole you've never
worn before.
And that is why when dogs meet, no matter
where they roam,
Each sniffs the other's arsehole in case it is his own.

I hope you don't need me to tell you that that's complete nonsense, since every arsehole being sniffed is actually its owner's personal calling card, combined with newsletter, health record and much more than time allows me to itemise. In any case, you probably wouldn't believe me even if I did.

The poem has only ever been spouted by the Boss when he's had a few glasses of that sheep's urine stuff he likes so much. I've always thought it's just as well he doesn't indulge all that often, because something in it makes him talk in a garbled sort of way and laugh at what he's saying, even when it isn't funny, like the ode to bahookie sniffing I've just quoted. Obviously, even a dog as quick on the uptake as me couldn't be expected to have a sufficiently extensive command of the human vocabulary to actually recite an entire poem, so I've had to rely on my interpreter to put the whole thing together from the basic outline I beamed over. Apparently, it's a fairly well-known ditty, so I trust it hasn't been too difficult for him.

The Boss said he learned it from someone in that 'separate activity' of his, the business interest I told you about that occasionally takes him away in some hope of boosting the Cuddy Neuk coffers. Yet nothing could have prepared me for the shock I got when eventually presented with an example of the actual business he was involved in…

*

THERE'S A PIG farm about half a mile from here, and the blood-curdling cacophony of squealing and screeching that comes out of it when there's a mass castration session in progress is beyond compare. Or so I thought.

It was early spring, and the calves that had been housed all winter were being let out to graze in a little grass paddock in front of the house. It's always been my favourite time of the year, springtime, when nature is re-born and there's new life blossoming, chirping, hopping, buzzing and fluttering all around. Young bucket-fed calves are great fun to watch when they're having their first experience of life outside the building they were reared in. Freedom! Sun-shiny, fresh-air-breathing, back-heeling, frolicking, leaping, bellowing, galloping freedom! If you've ever watched young calves being released into a grass field for the first time, you'll know what a spirit-lifting sight it is. As an expression of the sheer joy of being alive, it would be hard to beat. Fair enough, I know lambs do the same thing, and they're probably better than calves at the gambolling side of it – you know, the leaping in the air from a standing start sort of thing. I admit that's great to see as well, thinking back to my time at old Doddie's. But there are no sheep at Cuddy Neuk, just cattle, and there's no bigger thrill for me than to watch the young calves being let loose in the spring. And if I'm absolutely honest, even stolen moments of pleasure watching telly with the Boss don't really compare – not for an out-and-out nature girl like me at any rate.

Anyway, what happened was this...

There were a dozen or so calves, and I knew them all well, having been around them every day since they arrived from somewhere far away when only a week or two old. Why they'd been taken from their mothers always puzzled me. Maybe they were orphans. I don't know. I heard the Boss explaining it to the boys once: something to do with the farms they came from needing their mothers' milk for humans, but it made no sense to me. Anyhow, for calves like that, humans are the closest to mothers they ever get to know properly. And that's also how this little herd, like many before and after, got to know me: watching me watching them guzzling their milk out of bottles at first, then out of buckets once they'd got the knack of drinking without a teat. The bottle and bucket work was all done by Lady B and the Boss, of course, and they also had to nurse the calves and watch over them at all hours of the day and night if the poor wee critters weren't too well, which can often happen with young calves that come from somewhere far away like that.

So, knowing this little group as I did, I felt especially responsible for supervising them when they were given the freedom of the grass paddock in front of the house for the first time. They'd chase me too, just like the two orphan lambs I told you about at old Doddie's, and I'd make sure they didn't run slap-bang into a fence or hedge or something in the process. They're pretty stupid, young calves like that, when they get into a field with fences and hedges and things for the first time. They could hurt themselves pretty badly too, if they didn't have the likes of me controlling things. But it was all good fun anyway, and I was really enjoying myself until, all of a sudden, I heard this horrendous moaning and wailing and squealing. I could tell it was coming from back at the farm, and even though I was a fair distance away, the squealing hurt my ears. It really did.

The calves didn't seem bothered, though, so I waited until they'd settled down after the initial excitement of having their first taste of freedom, then made my way cautiously back to the farmyard. What greeted me there was really weird – frightening even. Let's be honest, it takes a lot to spook me. OK, that thunder stuff that sometimes explodes in the sky puts me in a right flap, which I freely admit. I mean, the first time I heard it I actually tried to dig my way into the farmhouse to escape. No kidding – I was digging away like mad under the kitchen window when Lady B came out and tried to calm me down. She blurted out something about electric flashes in the clouds, which was all gobbledegook to me, and I honestly don't think she actually knew what she was talking about herself. Humans are like that when they're trying to explain things they don't really understand. It's what the Boss calls 'bullshit', even when it has nothing to do with bulls or shit, like when politicians are on the telly, for example. But I'm digressing again, so let's get back to the moaning, wailing and squealing…

What greeted me when I poked my head round the corner of the cart shed and sneaked a peek into the yard was a woman dressed in a brightly checked skirt and shawl, with a big, black fur hat on her head. She was being attacked by a multi-legged creature that reminded me of one of those octopus things I'd seen on a natural world TV programme once. Except this octopus had rigid legs, with one of them stuck in the woman's mouth, and it had its body covered in a checked cloth that matched hers. Talk about weird! My first thought was that it was no wonder the poor soul was screaming. And then I noticed a group of men standing nearby and wondered why they didn't rush in and pull the monster off. After all, the woman was clearly in distress. Then, as suddenly as it had started, the wailing and screeching stopped, and the woman, cool and calm as you like, folded up her attacker and tucked it under her arm.

'Got all the pictures you need, boys?' came a deep voice from the mouth that had been occupied a moment earlier by the thin end of an octopus leg.

It was only then that I noticed the Boss, who seemed to be in charge of whatever was going on. He thanked the group of men, shook hands all round and saw them into their cars. Meanwhile, the woman with the deep voice busied herself taking the stiff octopus thing apart before stuffing it neatly into a case. Bizarre or what!

I was on the point of beating a hasty retreat, back to the normality of the calf paddock, when the deep voice rang out again – this time directed at me: 'Hello, boy! Well, you're a handsome chap, aren't you? Come on, then. Don't be shy. Come and say hello.' The voice had a friendly ring to it, and I was close enough to see that the eyes were beaming out favourable vibes too. Here was a genuine dog lover, and one who obviously appreciated good looks as well, so I reckoned I could forgive the mistaken assumption about my gender. After all, with such a poor sense of smell, humans have to rely on their eyesight when making such judgements, and I was pointing in the wrong direction for that.

All the same, I was still wary of this person, basically because that deep voice and the outlandish female garb didn't really go together. This was *very* weird, and it bothered me. But, cometh such a conundrum for a collie, cometh a collie's nature-given solution. I took a good sniff of the air drifting downwind towards me and – yes, you've guessed – it revealed that my new admirer was a man after all. That tell-tale male whiff I described to you earlier was there in abundance, its potency indicating that he'd only just dropped one, and also providing me with evidence, albeit superfluous, that he'd had a kipper for breakfast.

'Come on, boy,' he said again, then did the standard routine of patting his hands his on knees. 'Come and say hello.' Which I did, but demurely so, and still with an element of wariness as well. You can't be too careful when making friends with men dressed as women, or so the Boss had told me when watching one of them mincing about on telly one Christmas.

Anyway, it turned out that the man who took a shine to me in the Cuddy Neuk yard that day was no pantomime dame, but a bagpipe player of repute. For that's what he had been grappling with: a set of bagpipes, not a stiff-legged octopus in a checked shirt. And the piper's skirt wasn't a skirt either, but what Scotsmen call a 'kilt'.

This was all news to me, of course, and I wasn't really interested anyway. As soon as I learned that bagpipes were regarded as a musical instrument, I decided human beings were even stranger creatures than I'd already taken them for. Yet the Boss didn't regard the ear-splitting racket of bagpipes as mere music, but as the most stirring form of it imaginable: a source of pride to swell every Scotsman's heart – an uplift for his soul in times of despair – enough to bring tears to a glass eye in times of great joy. It seems he actually played the things himself in his youth, so it's as well he'd kicked the habit by the time I arrived at Cuddy Neuk, or I swear I'd have done a swift bunk to the relative tranquillity of the pig farm up the road.

What I didn't know at the time, however, was that the piper I'd chanced to meet was one of a whole band of pipers: Scots soldiers who specialised in guarding royal dragons and had made something called a record that had sold by the million all over the world. As far as I could make out, it was something that involved a piece of music about an amazing lady called Grace (whoever she was), and had been 'produced' by the Boss (whatever that meant). Anyway, this was regarded as a highly unusual thing for a farmer to have done, and that was why the piper had been brought to Cuddy Neuk to have his picture taken that day. Something like that anyway. But to be honest, I didn't understand what it was all about back then, and I still don't to this day.

What turned out to be the *really* amazing thing, though, was the outcome of that piper's reaction to my good looks. He thought I was great (well, he *was* only human, after all) and was desperate to find out where the Boss had bought me and if there might be another one like me for sale there. He was duly given instructions on how to get to old Doddie's place, and left, grinning like the cat that got the cream – or even a dead sparrow.

I immediately put the incident out of my mind, and got on with my bagpipe-free life of keeping an eye on cud-chewing cattle, soil-scratching hens, coming-and-going vehicles and also the sheep that frequently grazed the field on the other side of the road. I think I've already told you that Lady B had given me strict instructions when I arrived at Cuddy Neuk never to go near those sheep, for the very valid reason that they belonged to a neighbouring farmer, who had collies eminently capable of 'tending' the sheep without assistance from me; and also because venturing over that busy road would be to risk life and limb. I'd always respected her wishes, though the temptation to treat those well-tended sheep of farmer Jack's to a bit of fun was always there. And the opportunity to do just that eventually presented itself – quite unexpectedly and, I'm pleased to relate, totally unpremeditated by me.

*

THERE'S AN OLD carters' road that runs along the full length of the lower side of the farm, bounded by a hedge that had long since become interwoven with the remains a derelict wire fence. The chances of keeping the fence stock proof by periodically patching up the most 'porous' sections had ultimately decreased to such an extent that renewing it in its entirety became a necessity. It was a task the Boss applied himself to at the start of winter that same year, when all the cattle were safely housed and the old fence could be hauled out ready for replacement posts to be thumped in and strung with strands of new wire.

I used to enjoy accompanying the Boss when he was working on the fence, although the physical effort required made me feel exhausted – on his behalf, if you see what I mean. I suppose what I'm saying is that some humans *make* work for themselves by doing things for animals that do nothing but lie about in their sheds all winter being hand fed by the same humans who are out in all weathers renewing fences to keep them secure come summer while they're lying about chewing the cud in the field with the new fence. No, honestly, I felt sorry for the Boss failing to realise he was being taken for a mug. Can you imagine the cattle doing the same for him? No, I don't think so, and that's yet another reason I keep saying humans never fail to amaze me.

Still, I did enjoy going with him when he was busy fencing. Obviously, I avoided watching him actually *doing* the work, but it was nice sitting beside him when he took a break to have a snack and a fag. He always lobbed me a bit of his sandwich. Corned beef was my favourite, although the sour pickle stuff he had on it one time almost made me puke. But all things considered, I did enjoy those times, and you could always depend on the Boss having one of his little chats about whatever happened to be on his mind. It was usually way beyond me, but I sat and looked interested anyway, and that kept him happy.

Anyhow, this one particular day, when we were sitting there behind the hedge like that, a sheep came into the field through a gateway from the old road about fifty yards away. I could hardly believe my eyes! Then another sheep came through, and another and another, until there were about forty of them, all standing about looking lost and gormless, the way sheep do when they suddenly find themselves somewhere they haven't been before. A few seconds later, three Border collies came through the gate, crouching low as they took up position at separate points around the flock. A tall, elderly man then entered the field through the same gate.

'Ah,' said the Boss, 'that'll be Jack bringing some sheep to graze that young grass of ours in the far field. Good! They'll get it all nibbled down nicely before the frosts have a chance to nip it.' He grinned as he raised a hand to salute our neighbour, who acknowledged with a wave of his shepherd's crook while shouting a couple of commands to his dogs.

I was in a spin, unable to fully grasp what was happening. But after a few moments it began to dawn on me that the sheep now standing on *our* land were the same ones I'd frequently eyed up on farmer *Jack*'s land over the road. The same ones – or their near relatives – that Lady B had warned me never to cross the road to visit. The same ones – or their near relatives – that I'd long had a hankering to have a bit of fun with. Now here, at last, was an out-of-the-blue opportunity too good to pass up.

Apart from the surroundings, it was as if I was back at old Doddie's. Jack's dogs had all the same moves as Doddie's, his commands were the same too, although I didn't discern a single swear word – not from Jack, at any rate. I had a feeling it mightn't be long before the Boss put that discrepancy right, though.

The object of the exercise for Jack was to move his flock diagonally across the field to a gate in the far corner that opened into the field of young grass that would provide clean grazing for the next couple of weeks or so. Those first few words of command he'd given his dogs had set things going in textbook fashion. Jack's dogs knew what they were doing all right, and Jack himself was obviously a shepherd of considerable skill. I don't mind admitting that I actually stood enthralled for a few seconds, admiring the flawless execution of the task in hand, marvelling at the understanding that existed between man and dog, and no less the respect that the sheep had for both. These were elements of 'working' a bunch of sheep that I'd witnessed countless times before, of course, but they'd been so commonplace at old Doddie's that I'd never really paused to fully appreciate the beauty of it all. If there was such a thing as poetry in motion, this surely was it.

Ah, but were they having fun? I doubted it, so decided to remedy the situation in the way I'd tried and tested to perfection. I sensed the Boss had anticipated something dramatic was about to happen, but I made a dash for it before he had a chance to grab my collar. The trick had always been to startle the sheep into breaking ranks before the duty dogs twigged what was going on, which always resulted in at least a handful of the mob heading for the hills – figuratively speaking – and, with any luck, in totally different directions as well. That was when the real fun had always started for me, lying low and watching a well-drilled operation rapidly degenerate into a total shambles. And it looked as though the expected pattern of events was in the process of starting again, when two of Jacks' dogs, without any prompting from him, rapidly headed off the escapees while the third dog patrolled the flock, single-handedly discouraging any others from attempting to follow suit.

This was team playing of the highest order, an object lesson in how to control herd indiscipline that even old Doddie would readily have acknowledged. Now, I'm not saying that Jack and his dogs were any better at the job than old Doddie and his team, because that would be unfair. For all his quirks and foibles, Doddie really was second to none in the shepherding stakes, and the boasts he made about the proficiency of his dogs were totally justified too. No, what I saw as the main contributing factor in the failure of this attempt to emulate past promotions of fun was the fact that these lowland sheep were somehow less adventurous than their upland cousins. I certainly didn't put it down to any lack of technique on my part. I mean, I had nothing to prove in that regard anyway, and my presence being more or less ignored by Jack and his dogs could only have been intended as a mark of respect. In any event, the bottom line was that if those daft sheep didn't want to grab a few minutes of freedom from their humdrum existence, then why should I care?

With my tail held high, I casually made my way back to the Boss, who was still standing where I'd left him. It took but a glance at his face, however, to realise that he didn't see eye to eye with me on the finer points of this non-event. And the language he greeted me with would certainly have made old Doddie raise an approving thumb.

What the bloody hell had I thought I was doing, diving headlong at a flock of placid sheep like that?

Hadn't I the common sense to realise what a damned mess I might have made of things – a well-ordered, tightly-controlled group of sheep being suddenly turned into a panicking muddle – heading everywhere except where they were supposed to? And what, he wanted to know, would have happened if there had been any pregnant ewes among them? 'Jesus H. Christ, Jen,' he snapped, 'scaring the shit out of them like that could have made them abort!' He took a deep breath, looked heavenward and muttered, 'Yeah, and how do you think this makes *me* look?'

I sat gazing up at him, wearing my best 'Little Miss Innocent' look.

He stood staring back at me for a few moments, his expression grim. Then a sort of resigned look came to his face and he added with a shrug, 'Free spirit? Honest, Jen, if I'd had a gun a coupla minutes ago, I'd've fuckin' shot you!'

Well, if I could, I would have laughed out loud. Who was he kidding? He was nothing if not a compassionate man at heart, never one to deliberately hurt *any*one's feelings, and he knew well enough how upset I got when I heard loud bangs. The Boss shoot *me*? Not a chance. No, what was *really* bothering him wasn't my attempt to scatter Jack's sheep – after all, they'd come to no harm – but rather that he'd lost face as a dog handler in front of a master of the craft. The truth of the matter was, you see, that the only sound to be heard during the entire episode was the Boss yelling:

'JEN! … COME BACK! … COME BACK *HERE*! … JEN! … *JE-E-E-N*! … COME BACK HERE

RIGHT *NOW*, YA HOOR!'

As I'd done as a matter of course when being shouted at by old Doddie, I took my own good time to do the Boss's bidding. Yet I understood how he felt – sort of – so I resolved there and then never to get up to such mischief again. There would be plenty of other ways to enjoy myself without embarrassing the Boss. Of that there was absolutely no doubt at all in my mind.

*

LADY B WAS waiting for us when we got back to the farmyard that evening. Not surprisingly, the Boss didn't let on about the wee drama that had temporarily interrupted his fencing operations earlier in the day. The last thing he'd have wanted to do was admit that he'd shown himself up to be a failure as a dog handler in front of our old neighbour. And anyway, it would have been a pity to put a damper on the happy mood that Lady B was clearly in. She was grinning from ear to ear as she presented the Boss with a piece of paper.

'Look – look at this. It's a letter about Jen's brother – or half-brother, or whatever – the one old Doddie sold to that Pipe Major chap who was here having his picture taken a while back. This is from him.'

The somewhat glum look that had been darkening the Boss's features gradually morphed into a smile, and a highly delighted one at that. 'Who'd have believed it?' he said, shaking his head. 'Not just the pipe band's mascot, but a celebrity with the general public over there as well, it says here.'

Lady B handed him a photograph. 'Yes, and look at this. This is him marching with the band – up there by the Pipe Major's side. Imagine that! Jen's brother marching in the front row of a pipe band – and such a famous one as that as well! And look – look at his markings – he's Jen's double!'

The Boss continued to smile and shake his head as he read the rest of the letter out loud. As usual, most of what he said meant little or nothing to me, but the gist of it seemed to be that the dog, my semi-sibling, was called Jock Grey – 'Jock' because he was Scottish, and the 'Grey' bit had something to do with his regiment (whatever that was) using grey horses. Why they didn't use tractors like everybody else wasn't explained – or if it was, I didn't get it. Anyway, this semi-sibling of mine had become a big deal because his owner – that bagpiper I thought at first was a woman being attacked by an octopus thing – was the boss bagpiper in the band that had that huge hit record about the amazing woman called Grace I told you about. And so he, Jock Grey, had become this big deal in the papers and on the telly and everything in the place where the regiment lived: a place called Germany, which I think is quite far away. It's a bit beyond Gifford somewhere, unless I misunderstood what the Boss said.

Whatever, the Boss and Lady B were all smiles about it and said old Doddie would be really pleased, and I should also be proud of my half-brother, particularly as he looked so much like me. And yes, truth to tell, I did feel pretty chuffed when they showed me that picture of him marching with all those bagpipers. Mind you, I couldn't help feeling a bit sorry for him as well, since it was obvious the poor bugger must have been born deaf!

* * * * *

– *ELEVEN* –

DID I EVER tell you my memory isn't as good as it used to be? Anyway, it isn't, which is the thing about getting a wee bit older: you sometimes forget things you used to remember. What's weird, though, is I can still remember things from years and years ago, while I occasionally forget what's just happened. Strange. But then again, when you think about it – if you can't remember something, how do you know you forgot it in the first place? That's what *I*'d like to know. I'll have to think about it sometime … if I remember.

Not that I'm too worried about being a bit forgetful. That said, there *have* been a couple of occasions when things didn't work out as well as they otherwise would, and I must confess they *did* bother me.

The first one would have been just about a year ago, I think, and sort of linked back to that dog show I once saw on the telly. You know, the one with the Afghan Hound that won the Supreme Champion prize. I'm talking about big Boris – the classy one – him that pissed on the judge's shoe – him I fancied rotten. And the other dog I told you about was the

Border collie that won a prize for going fast over jumps and through pipes and stuff like that. It didn't do a flying back flip, though. Remember what I'm talking about now? Well, what happened was this…

IT WAS A nice, sunny day during the summer and nothing much was going on about the place. I'd spent some time keeping myself busy watching a bunch of young heifers lying about chewing the cud in that wee paddock in front of the house. Then I checked on the hens pecking and scraping around in their run. That's one thing about hens – they keep pecking and scraping, even when it's a lazy kind of sunny day and nobody else can be bothered doing much except chew the cud, if you're that way inclined, or maybe just have a quiet snooze. Which is what I must have done after I was satisfied the hens were doing all right. When I say 'must have done', what I mean is that I couldn't actually remember falling asleep outside the hen run, and I also couldn't remember going from the hen run back to the field with the heifers in it. But that's where I woke up – back in the wee paddock, I mean. And I woke up with a real start, believe me. In fact, I honestly couldn't believe what was happening. It was like I was still asleep and having my worst nightmare. It really was. The shock must have jolted my memory, though, because it all began to come back to me then. Talk about wishing I was dead! Honestly, I was sorry the Boss hadn't shot me after that little 'episode' we had with farmer Jack's sheep.

But I was still very much alive, and having to cope with a situation that truly was a fate worse than death for a dog who'd spent her life upholding impeccable moral values, never mind maintaining equally select 'social barriers'. You see, when I came to in the wee paddock, my nether regions were firmly joined to those belonging to a dog of the opposite sex. In case you haven't quite grasped the picture, we're talking here about a bahookie-to-bahookie situation, which indicated – not to put too fine a point on it – that I'd been humped. Well and truly shafted, and left in that ungainly physical position that dogs occasionally find themselves in when a certain post-hump spasm occurs. I'd seen a few of my seniors get into the same mess back at old Doddie's, so I knew right away what had happened.

However, the big question was, 'With whom?' And just as crucially, 'How?'

While still in a hazy, half-awake state, like the one you experience when coming out of a deep sleep, my initial thought was that I'd been having a 'tryst' with none other than Boris the beautiful Afghan. As you know, I'd often dreamed of having such amorous liaisons with him, and this manifestation of the dream, which was super realistic by the way, had taken place in the feed passage of the cattle shed, all specially done up for the occasion with lots of fresh, fluffy straw and sparkly lights all over the place. It was a bit like one of those singing and dancing programmes you see on TV sometimes. Anyway, we were really having a right good go, when – just as we were hitting the high note, so to speak – I suddenly had this really uncomfortable feeling in the bahookie region. And that's when I came to and found myself in the wee paddock, locked in that ungainly position I was just describing.

Instinctively, I tried to turn round to find out who the other half of the coupling was, but the very nature of that predicament prevents you from seeing any farther back than your own shoulder. Even so, I realised pretty damned quick that it wasn't Boris the Afghan. Although I had never had the pleasure of sampling his personal scent, it took but the briefest of backwards sniffs to tell me I hadn't been humped by him. For there was only one dog I knew who stank like that, and the moment this realisation hit me was the moment I wished I was dead.

How could I have allowed that scruffy fleabag Shuggie from up the road to get away with this? How, after all those years of having his approaches thwarted, had he finally managed to succeed where all other no-hopers had failed? The scary thing was that I couldn't remember. Yet details of everything I'd done earlier that day were still as fresh in my memory as when they'd taken place.

I felt I'd been led up the proverbial garden path *and* taken for a ride – literally. But more than anything else, I was stunned by the thought that I had absolutely no recollection of how this had come about. And as if my self esteem hadn't been bruised enough already, the Boss was about to sink his own boot in for good measure.

I presume he must have been looking out from the yard and noticed what appeared to be a huge, hairy crab sidestepping jerkily across the wee paddock and making for the nearest hedge, which is what dogs do to cover their embarrassment in these circumstances. I also remembered this from my youth at old Doddie's, when I'd thought such scenes to be really funny. I couldn't understand how the culprits could be stupid enough to make such fools of themselves. But now that I'd found myself in the same predicament, I was learning the hard way that there's nothing remotely amusing about it. Being caught in a copulative contraction is a serious business – and damned painful too, let me tell you.

You already know what I thought about the threat of being given a bath, and I still count myself lucky for having avoided that ordeal. Yet it may well have been a lot less shocking than having a bucket of ice-cold water chucked over me. For that's what the Boss did, and I couldn't have been more grateful to him, albeit that I was absolutely mortified as well. Having a length of baler twine tied to my collar was the first time I'd been on anything remotely resembling a lead, but the Boss was obviously making sure I wouldn't revert to whatever wayward ways had led me into the fix he'd just freed me from. I understood that, and was resigned to accepting the penalty of humiliation that went with it.

What really rankled, though, was having to stand there looking on as that reprobate Shuggie gave himself a brisk shake, cocked his leg against a cud-chewing heifer, then swaggered off homeward with a glint in his eye and a spring in his step that were clearly intended to let me know that the long wait had been well worthwhile. What a pretentious upstart! What a devious, impertinent arsehole!

IRONICALLY, THE BEST thing to do after such an unforgettable experience is to try and forget it as quickly as possible. Easier said than done for most, I suppose, but no great problem for me. Or so I told myself as I got on with my daily routine of overseeing the livestock, protecting the property, playing with the boys, seeing off unwelcome visitors (particularly male dogs!) and generally keeping the Boss and Lady B happy. Then, a few weeks later, I noticed Lady B looking at me in a knowing sort of way. I knew what she was thinking, because I was having exactly the same thought myself. It's a female 'thing', which I was already aware existed between bitches and ewes and cows, but hadn't realised was also shared by humans. But as I'd sussed on the very first day we met, Lady B was more perceptive than she looked. That, as you may recall, was when she'd clocked me eyeing up farmer Jacks' sheep on the other side of the road, and lectured me about not going near them. Well, this time neither the sheep nor the road featured in her observation, which focused instead on my rear end, though the presence or otherwise of dangleberries was now of no concern.

'A wee bit of a dribble there, Jen?' she said. 'Hmm, you're probably too old for the obvious, but I think we'll get the vet to have a look at you anyway – just in case.'

I knew within myself that no confirmation would be needed from any vet, but Lady B was doing her best as usual, which I appreciated. If I'm honest, I suppose the only thing I'd have wanted from a vet at that stage would have been a cure for memory lapse, but I had a hunch this might be beyond human ingenuity – and even if it wasn't, it would have been a bit bloody late to make any difference by then.

It was the first time I'd ever been examined by a vet, although I'd watched them doing their various things with cattle often enough. Things like helping cows that were having trouble calving; burning horn 'buds' off calves heads; separating male calves from their testicles; snipping tiny nipples off female calves that had a few more than the desired four; inserting rings through young bulls' noses. Things like that, and some of them a bit gruesome to watch, as you can imagine. For instance, I've seen vets with an arm up to the shoulder in cows' bahookies sometimes. I mean, how gruesome is that! And not too pleasant for the cows either, I dare say.

'It's all right, Jen – nothing to worry about. Just gonna have a wee feel at your tummy, that's all.' So said Jim the vet as he knelt down beside me in the yard here, with the Boss and Lady B in fascinated attendance. I liked Jim, and he liked me. I knew this from the way he always spoke to me first when he arrived, no matter which humans were around as well. You can always trust a person who has the manners to talk to the dog first. I've always stuck by that belief and it hasn't let me down yet. Anyhow, I noticed Jim wasn't toting any knives or hot irons or even a bucket of disinfectant on this occasion, so I was prepared to take him at his word when he said I had nothing to worry about. I did have *slight* doubts about his use of the word 'nothing', though.

'Aye, it'd be unlikely at her age' he muttered,

prodding my body here and there. 'Twelve, you say?'

'About that,' the Boss replied.

'Going on thirteen now,' said Lady B.

Jim produced a rolled up tube contraption from his pocked, stuck two bits of it in his ears and pressed the other end against my belly.

'Hear anything?' said the Boss, cupping a hand to his own ear.

Jim raised a forefinger to indicate that silence was required. He moved the end of the tube contraption around a bit, then stood up with a look on his face that was a mix of surprise and admiration. 'Well, there's *some*thing in there all right.'

'You mean...?' the Boss and Lady B enquired in unison.

Jim looked down at me and gave a little smile. 'When did you say she, ehm ... did the deed?'

'About six weeks ago,' said the Boss. 'Right out of character too. But that's what she'd been up to all right. Had to do the old bucket of water routine to unglue them, if you know what I mean.'

'Always does the trick,' said Jim, grinning at me. 'No fool like an old fool, eh lass?'

That remark disappointed me. Old, fair enough, but a *fool*? No, I'd taken Jim to be a better judge of character than that. And it had also been a bit off to assure me that I had 'nothing to worry about', only to go through all his vet-type rigmarole to confirm what Lady B and I instinctively knew anyway: I was up the duff, and six weeks down the road at that.

'Yeah, she is a bit long in the tooth to be having her first litter,' Jim said as he was preparing to leave, 'but she's a fine healthy specimen – hardy as they come – so she'll cope fine, I'm sure.' He glanced down at me and winked. 'Just as long as you enjoyed yourself. That's the main thing, Jen.'

En*joy*ed myself! Enjoyed being humped by a mangy cur that I normally wouldn't have allowed within sniffing distance? No chance! But in fairness to the vet, how was he to know the circumstances? I mean, I would have had to rely on the Boss to convey that information, and even he didn't know the truth. How could he? And to complicate matters even further, I couldn't deny that I *had* actually enjoyed 'doing the deed', albeit that I'd thought I was doing it with the dog of my dreams.

OK, fair enough, so maybe the vet was right after all: maybe there *is* no fool like an old fool, although it pains me to admit it. It all comes down to being absent-minded, of course, and as I say, there *was* another instance that bothered me, though only when I became aware of the details which, needless to say, I couldn't remember at the time. But that happened quite a while after the first lapse, and I had more than enough to concentrate on in the meantime…

*

NOBODY MADE A fuss of me following the vet's visit, and I was pleased about that. It was my own business, and I'd mind it in the way nature intended – by doing what came naturally. I knew female intuition helped Lady B recognise this, and I'm sure she must have advised the others accordingly, because the usual invitations to play football rapidly ceased, as did any encouragement from the Boss to hop up on the trailer when he was going off to fetch turnips or whatever for the cattle. However, for all that they weren't molly-coddling me, I could tell they *were* keeping a discreet eye on me, and help would have been immediately at hand if I'd needed it. But I didn't. Much as I appreciated their concern, I'd got myself into this situation without assistance from anyone, so it was up to me to see my own way out of it as well. That's another great quality we Border collies have – we're nothing if not independent.

I WON'T DWELL on how I felt when my one and only little pup was born, but I guess it would have been no different from how a mother of any species would feel. I licked him all over, nuzzled him and nudged him gently with my nose, hoping against hope that I'd be able to kindle the spark of life. But it wasn't to be.

I caught sight of Lady B watching me from a distance when I carried the wee fellow away; off to a quiet spot I knew along the old road, near where the Boss and I had often sat and spent some rest time when he was working on that new fence. There was a place there where I knew he'd be safe, where no prying fox would disturb him. I tried not to think too much of what might have been, of how he would have looked when he'd grown a bit. Maybe, if he'd been lucky, he'd have looked just like me; but in fairness, perhaps with just a touch of Shuggie about him too. Not in appearance, mark you, but hopefully with some of his father's dour determination. That wouldn't have been too bad a quality to inherit. I'll give the old bugger that. But I'd never know, and there was nothing I could do but accept that this was nature's way, and it wasn't for me to even try and understand.

Afterwards, it would have been easy, and maybe understandable, for the Boss and Lady B to have smothered me in sympathy, and doubtless many in their position would have done just that. But I was glad they didn't. Make no mistake, though – dogs have feelings just like humans, and none more deeply felt than grief, even for the loss of a tiny stillborn puppy like mine. But as Jim the vet had pointed out, I come from hardy stock, and being a typical Border collie it's in my nature to be resilient in the face of adversity.

Having said all that, I confess to having felt the need of *some* help in getting over what had been a traumatic and, in the end, a very lonely experience. But I was fortunate in that my little pack of humans understood and gave me all the support necessary in the most sympathetic yet undemonstrative of ways. And there was no better exponent than Lady B herself. For instance, if she chanced to see me around the steading somewhere – perhaps coming away from one of my supervisory visits to the cattle shed – she would beckon me to come and sit next her on a straw bale or something, then she'd lay her hand on my head and stroke it gently for a while. Not a single word was spoken.

As you know, we had exchanged many thoughts

over the years, and not all of them on the same wavelength either. But the empathy that flowed between us at moments such as this was, I believe, as profound and enduring as could be shared by two mothers of any species. And I understood why...

*

IT HAPPENED ONE morning about a year after I came here. The boys had set out as usual on the short walk up the road to catch the school bus. After seeing them off at the gate, the Boss and Lady B had gone back inside the house, and I was mooching about the yard doing nothing in particular. It was a beautifully calm morning, with just a hint of sea in the air, and nothing to be heard but the chattering of sparrows in the hedgerows and the faint groan of a tractor working in a field somewhere down towards the coast. It was what I'd come to think of as the start of a typically peaceful Cuddy Neuk day, and I was about to make the most of it by lying down in a sunny spot against the byre wall, when the stillness was broken by the sound of a car coming down the road at speed. Then I heard the screech of skidding tyres, followed by an eerie silence.

I never saw little Boy Two again, and it was feared Boy One might not survive the injuries he'd sustained either. In a fleeting moment, the simple gifts of nature had been torn away and replaced with dark clouds of shock and disbelief. As a young dog, I didn't understand what had happened at first, but though my familiarity with their emotions was still limited,

I knew from the looks on the Boss and Lady B's faces that something very bad had happened.

The following days and weeks passed in a strangely quiet way. Come what may, livestock have to be fed and crops tended, and perhaps the knowledge that other living things depended on them for survival was what kept the Boss and Lady B going through those bleak times. As for me, all I could do to comfort them was what all dogs do if we sense something is troubling our human friends: I sat close beside them, rested my chin on Lady B's lap and looked into her eyes, in the same way that, years later, she would soothe my own feelings of loss by gently stroking my head.

But while I had no way of knowing it then, I'm sure that what sustained them more than anything else would have been their hope that the fragile cord of life to which Boy One was clinging would hold out.

And it did.

* * * * *

– TWELVE –

YOU'LL PROBABLY RECALL how I mentioned that no big fuss was made of me after I'd lost my one and only pup. Everyone tried to make life seem as normal as possible, knowing this was the best way to help me get over what had happened. Well, that's also how things were some nine or ten years earlier, when Boy One came back from a place they called 'the hospital'. I think he was still only about eight in human years, so just a kid, really. When he got out of the car in the yard, the first thing he did was call me over and give me a hug, exactly as he'd done the day we first met. But now he had the same look in his eyes that I'd seen in Boy Two's on that same occasion: a look that had told me the little fellow was disappointed because I wasn't exactly like Muffet, their previous dog. I'd sensed immediately back then that Muffet was deeply missed by both boys, just as Boy One was feeling the loss of his wee brother now.

I could only imagine how he must have felt, but instead of making a show of sympathy, I deliberately did all I could to make him smile. I'd perform my stone-catching trick with even bigger stones than before; I'd make a more spectacular tyre-worrying show than ever when seeing vehicles off the premises; I'd dazzle him afresh with my football dribbling skills; and I'd even try to make him laugh by skidding around the yard on my bahookie – but only, I must stress, when Lady B wasn't looking. And sure enough, little by little, things did begin to return to *some*thing like normal.

Then, about a year later, Lady B went away for a couple of days and came back with a new baby – a male one. I'd never seen such a small human before, and I must confess I thought he looked pretty much the same as a new-born rabbit, or even my own pup – except bigger, of course, and with a different smell. I've already told you what I regard as the defining scent of the human male, and all I can add is that baby ones smell even worse than the rest. I mean, no wonder they need to have those things that look like clip-on underpants mucked out every day. Quite frankly, I'd never have gone for a roll in the midden again if I'd thought *that* stuff was being dumped in it.

Of course, the arrival of *New* Boy Two (for that's what I called him) had come as no great surprise to me, because that female 'thing' I've talked about had alerted me to Lady B's condition well in advance. I'd then gone out of my way to do nothing that might annoy or upset her, which is why, for instance, I made sure she wasn't looking when I entertained Boy One to performances of arse-wiping on gravel. Oh yes indeed, a dog with a nature as selfless as mine must be prepared to tread a tricky tightrope at times. But then again, you wouldn't expect anything less from your best friend, would you?

* * *

HUMANS SAY A year in a dog's life is equivalent to seven of theirs, which means we grow old faster than they do, by *their* reckoning at any rate. Humans also say that dogs have no concept of time, although I'm not sure what they mean by that. I mean, OK, dogs don't have clocks or watches, so we don't see time in terms of minutes or hours, or any other bunches of time that humans use to organise their lives around. Time for dogs is now, this very moment, and we live our lives for that. Yesterday's gone, and the next second may not even happen, never mind tomorrow.

On the other hand, maybe it's just that humans think we don't have any concept of the *passage* of time, but that's only correct in so much as we don't define it in those silly measures, which mean nothing, because they don't exist. Not like smells, or tastes or things you can look at anyway. But make no mistake, we *are* conscious of time passing: like how it can make us anxious, or even pine, if our humans go away for longer than usual, or impatient if our food isn't dished up when our bellies tell us it should. But what I'm trying to say is that we're not *slaves* to time, so are therefore more free than you are, if you see what I mean. I mean, you're the ingenious ones, so work it out for yourselves, for Christ's sake! What do I know? I'm only a dumb animal.

Anyhow, what I was thinking about when I got

sidetracked onto the subject of time was how quickly it passed after New Boy Two came on the scene. It seemed that no sooner had he stopped having those underpants things emptied out every so often than he was scooting about on a bike, joining in football games with Boy One and me, and then going off to school every day. He used to giggle at my bahookie-scraping routine as well, but I only showed him a few times, firstly because I still didn't want to risk being caught in the act by Lady B, and secondly because the older I got myself the less my backside could take it. What's that saying of yours – the mind is willing but the body refuses to cooperate? Something like that. Still, going by the smell, I'm pretty sure he peed his pants laughing at that stunt, just as little Boy Two had done before him, and I got a real kick from that. It sort of helped make a happy link from the past to the present, if you see what I mean.

It was probably about the same time that I also quit lobbing stones in the air and catching them in my mouth. It wasn't that New Boy Two didn't show his appreciation as much as everyone else, but simply because, like my bahookie, my teeth had started to object. As I've said before, it gets to the stage that the reward no longer justifies the pain.

Maybe it was pure coincidence, or maybe it was because the boys missed my stone-catching stuff, but before long a contraption they called *Swing Ball Tennis* appeared on the patch of grass at the side of the house. I'd already seen them playing a game they called simply *Tennis,* which involved bashing a ball to and fro over a piece of rope tied between two clothes poles. To be honest, it seemed a pretty pointless exercise to me, and totally boring too. Not being physically suited to wielding one of the 'racket' things they used for hitting the ball, all I could do was lie about waiting for one of the boys to miss it or clatter it under a bush or something, then I'd fetch it and drop it at their feet. A silly game indeed, but it amused the boys, so I didn't mind doing my bit.

But this *Swing Ball* version was different. It consisted of a pole about the same height as the Boss, with a length of string tied to the top and a tennis ball attached to the other end. What the boys did was stand a few paces apart at opposite sides of the pole and hit the ball to each other with little bat things, which I soon worked out was not the intended object of the game. This was clearly meant as a substitute for extreme stone catching, and while I was genuinely grateful that the boys had made such a thoughtful gesture, I felt disinclined to play ball – literally. Here was a human invention intended for the amusement of wimpy lapdogs, and I was certainly *not* one of those. However, never one to deliberately hurt feelings, I went along with the boys' interpretation of the game for a while, deftly nodding the ball back to one or the other whenever it swung near me. They seemed impressed, and not at all disappointed that I wasn't actually catching it. Humans never fail to amaze me – not being able to grasp the rules of even a simple ball-catching game. Anyway, after a few weeks my patience finally gave out and I leapt up, grabbed the ball in mid swing and worried its string to shreds with my teeth – or what was left of them.

Then, mission accomplished, I picked the ball up and casually dropped it at the boys' feet, with a look that said, 'There you are – now you can have a *proper* game of tennis.' They didn't seem all that happy, though, which surprised me, but just goes to show how difficult it can be to please humans at times.

* * *

IT COULD HAVE been the onset of what you might call middle age (Lady B said I was seven in human years, which was the equivalent of about fifty for a dog), but for the first time since adopting my fun-focused outlook on life when still a youngster, I woke up one morning with a strange urge to do a bit of work. No, honestly, I mean real *work*, not just moseying about checking on cattle and hens and doing all the other odds and ends about the place that I regarded as a piece of cake. Or a walk in the park, to borrow a more dog-slanted example from the list of silly human sayings I've heard over the years.

As luck would have it, the Boss had chosen that particular day to move a bunch of heifer stirks to a nearby field that he rented for grazing every summer. (Heifer *stirks*, if you want to know, is what farmers call yearling female cattle – or the cow equivalent of teenage girls.) The plan, as ever, was to drive them along the road 'on the hoof', an operation from which I'd always been excluded, since my staying behind to keep an eye on things was a much more vital task. Well, that's what the Boss had always told me, and as I'm never one to shirk responsibility, I'd always been happy to oblige. But if you want to know the truth, I spent most of the time snoozing in my favourite sun trap against the byre wall, undisturbed by anyone, except maybe an occasional sales rep, who'd be seen off without even daring to get out of his car.

Old Doddie had instilled in me a mistrust of what he referred to as 'them smarmy arseholes' when I was only a pup, and although I grew up to be the most hospitable dog you could ever meet, the compulsion to scare the shit out of these guys has never left me. It's wonderful the effect a flurry of barking, snarling, baring teeth, biting car door handles, kicking up gravel, foaming at the mouth (simulated, of course!) and generally acting like a complete maniac has on the average sales rep. His only retaliation as he accelerates towards the gate will be a barrage of insults yelled from behind a tightly closed window: '*Collies*? *You're all the bloody same – stark, ravin', fuckin' mad*!'

I love it!

But thoughts of hounded salesmen and sneaky snoozes were far from my mind on this particular morning. As usual, the Boss had told me to stay in the yard and do my guard dog thing while the mini cattle drive was taking place, and I thought it prudent to give the impression that I would do just that. Better to hang back, I reckoned, until I could work out how best to offer my assistance. Then fate intervened in the most unexpected of ways...

The heifer stirks had been herded into a corral between the cattle shed and the hen run, ready for heading off to their summer grazings as soon as the Boss had given them a final once-over. So far, so good.

Meanwhile, Lady B had finished gathering the eggs and was almost back at the kitchen door, when she shouted to the Boss: 'Check the gate of the hen run, will you? Hands full – had to pull it shut with my foot.'

Too late. To reach the gate, the Boss had to make his way from the far side of the hen run, and before he was even half way across, six of the most observant of the hens had already completed their bid for freedom, with the remaining half dozen tiptoeing briskly behind. 'Stop them quick!' he bellowed at Lady B. 'If they get into the veg garden, they'll trash everything!'

Too late again. The little plot where the Boss grew his potatoes and cabbages and stuff just happened to be easily visible through the wire netting of the hen run, and therefore covetously eyed by the inmates on a permanent basis. Hens, in case you don't know, do have a taste for fresh greens, so here was an opportunity too good for them to miss. It also just happened that the Boss's young lettuce plants were at their most succulent stage, and within seconds their lovingly tended rows were buried under a flapping whirlwind of leaf-ripping beaks and dirt-scraping claws. It's amazing that gentle birds like chickens can be so violent when they're in a lettuce-induced feeding frenzy. I'd never seen anything like it. I mean, you wouldn't want to be a worm, and the noise was pretty shocking too. It actually reminded me of the din I'd heard one night at old Doddie's when a fox got into his hen house. No kidding, it was as bad as that, and all over some boring vegetables that not even the most ill-bred of dogs would scrap over. Hens! They never fail to puzzle me, they really don't.

I'd never had occasion to see hens being rounded up before, so it had never occurred to me that the most important difference between hens and sheep and cattle is that hens can fly – not all that well, admittedly, but a helluva lot better than a collie. That being the case, and in spite of the fact that I had this urge to do a bit of real work, I had a feeling it might be better to sit this one out. What finally decided me, though, was the sight of the Boss, Lady B *and* both boys suddenly appearing together and running about like the proverbial headless chickens in a desperate, though inevitably futile, effort to get all the hens back into their run. I didn't hang about to see the full performance, but went for a lie down in my wee house instead. Sometimes discretion is the better part of helpfulness – or something.

The conclusion of this incident was that those hens that *were* eventually re-captured were never seen again, after being bundled into crates and driven off in a truck belonging to a neighbouring poultry farmer. He specialised in selling eggs, by the way, as opposed to oven-ready chickens ... I *think*.

*

THE HULLABALOO CAUSED by the hens rubbishing the veg garden hadn't long passed when an even worse one broke out. It's still a bit of a mystery how the two young bulls managed to get out of their pen and into the heifers' enclosure, particularly since two gates, three fences and the breeze block bulk of the cattle shed stood in their way. But when youthful male hormones are on the loose, nothing will keep their hosts from the door on which opportunity knocks. Which is why, from a livestock farmer's point of view, pubescent males and females are best kept apart, except under carefully controlled conditions. How else do you think humans got away with all that selective breeding stuff for so long? By the same token, allowing young females to mate too early can risk damaging their immediate well-being *and* longer-term breeding potential, which is bad business for the farmer. This is all well and good, but from a horny young bull's point of view, the only maxim to be followed would be: 'When they're big enough, they're old enough.' And this was the situation now prevailing in the heifers' enclosure.

Talk about mayhem! OK, you'd expect the bulls to waste no time in picking out their preferred mating targets, which would result in a fair amount of jostling for position on the part of those heifers most immediately inclined to be amenable. But when you include the fact that heifers are prone to mount each *other* as well, what quickly results is a scenario that I heard the Boss describe as 'a free-for-all bloody humpfest'. A strange expression, but I suppose he meant a sort of orgy, specifically one involving sex-crazed animals big enough to crush their human keepers to death without even realising they were there.

As soon as I saw the Boss and Lady B wading into the fray, I knew that fate had presented me with an ideal opportunity to satisfy my urge for a spot of real work.

'What the hell are *you* doing here?' the Boss yelled at me, clearly surprised that I was prepared to risk serious injury to help him in his moment of need. 'Bugger off!' he added sharply. Of course, I knew he was only thinking of my own safety, for which I was suitably grateful, but having made my decision, there would be no going back. That's the stuff us Border collies are made of.

All of these young cattle had been reared on the place, so were well accustomed to being in close contact with the Boss, Lady B and, most of all, with me, as I had kept a protective eye on them every day of their lives, even sleeping in their pens whenever I felt like it. I'd also had many moments of fun with them, pretending to be scared when they were in the mood to chase me out of their field. As you know, cattle are like that: always wanting to chase you out of their field. But circumstances were different now that they were bunched up in a confined space, and in the company of members of the opposite sex for the first time since realising there *was* such a thing.

Chaos reigned. Here was the natural force of pro-creation being pitted against human beings who chose to challenge its strength, and I don't deny the Boss and Lady B were showing that they were prepared to give the contest their best shots. But it also made me aware of how reckless humans can be when they get a bee in their bonnet about something. A bee in their bonnet? A wasps' nest in their underpants, more like! This was nothing short of risking broken bones at least, or death, if the best of good luck didn't pitch in on their side.

Anyway, I had committed myself to backing them up, so for starters I set about distracting the bulls from their main objective, and I did that by creating as much of a commotion as I could at the heels of whatever heifers they were about to familiarise themselves with. (I can't speak for humans, but all the animals I've known aren't too relaxed about humping when a dog is barking its head off round their ankles.) And my ploy was working well until the Boss started to wave his arms about and shout like a madman – not at the bulls and heifers, but at *me*, would you believe? Predictably, it only made matters worse.

It's just as well Lady B has more self-control than the Boss in such situations. I'd noticed this many times before, most recently during the battle of wits with the hens in the vegetable patch, when Lady B displayed her knack of taking a deep breath, remaining calm and refraining from any attempt to get the better of an agitated chicken by yelling swear words at it. She adopted the same technique now, coolly opening the wire-mesh gate between the corral and the empty hen run, and encouraging any heifers so inclined to pass through. It was a hit-and-miss procedure and never likely to solve the problem completely, but it did succeed in simplifying the action in the main arena. There were now only the two young bulls and a handful of the most 'flirty' of the heifers to contend with. Good thinking by Lady B, whose composure in the midst of turmoil made me think she'd have made a pretty good collie – apart from smelling like a fake flower, that is.

'Run to the bull pen and get two leads,' she shouted to Boy One, who had been watching the spectacle with his little brother from outside the corral. 'And be quick – while your father's still in one piece!'

The 'leads' she referred to were lengths of rope with a stout metal clip on one end for hooking through a bull's nose ring. Good thinking again. Even so, getting the leads attached to the bulls' noses was never going to be an easy task, especially when the objects of the exercise were focused on sampling as much as possible of the nubile wares on offer. But the Boss showed considerably more fleetness of foot than I'd ever seen him display before. I'll give him that, although I suppose prospects of becoming the filling in a bull-and-heifer sandwich would tend to bring out unplumbed reserves of agility in *any*one. But luck was on his side, and first one bull then the other was transformed from being a horny hulk of bulging muscle into nothing more aggressive than an overgrown pussycat. Bulls aren't inclined to make any false moves when being led by a rope attached to a ring through their noses. And neither would you be, if you think about it.

Anyway, while the Boss was getting on with that, I concentrated on helping Lady B coax the remaining heifers into the hen run: a task not without risk in itself. Whether it was a matter of familiarity breeding contempt, or simply that the heifers were piqued at having their temptress work-out interrupted is neither here nor there. All that matters is that my erstwhile friends did their best to butt and back-heel me into touch, and it took all of my ducking-and-diving skills to show them who was in charge. Well, fair enough, Lady B *did* help a bit in that regard with a persuasive 'tap' or two of a stick on the worst offenders' rumps.

It took a while for the dust to settle, but when calm had eventually descended on the scene, both bulls were tethered to the rails of the corral and the full complement of heifer stirks was safely enclosed in the hen run. And no matter what the Boss says to the contrary, I still maintain it wasn't my fault that chaos had reigned for so long. It's clear in my mind that over-excitement generated by the inadvertent presence of two young bulls among the heifers was at the root of the problem, and my barking at the culprits did no more harm than the Boss's shouting.

But that's the thing about some humans: when they've done something wrong, they've always got to blame the dog. I mean, a perfect example is the one I mentioned about human females dropping silent farts in company, then glancing accusingly at the family pet when the smell starts to circulate. When you think about it, it's the same thing with the Boss and his shouting – except louder, of course.

Anyhow, I decided I'd done enough real work for one day, and was more than pleased to remain behind when the heifers were being walked along the road to their summer grazing place. Frankly, it struck me that I'd been wrong to yield to the temptation of actually working in any case, and I certainly wouldn't succumb to the urge in a hurry again. I've stuck to that principle ever since. What's the point, when all's said and done, of knocking your pan out to help your human friends out of a jam if all you get in return is a mouthful of foul language and the finger of guilt?

But as luck would have it, a sales rep happened to blunder into the yard when the mini cattle drive was under way, so he bore the brunt of my frustrations as he was being harried off the property. It was the perfect way for me to let off steam, and I thoroughly enjoyed myself. Oh, and just to assure the Boss that I bore him no lasting grudge, I treated him to a perfect flying back flip as soon as he came back into the yard. For that's another thing about being Border collie: I'm too smart to cut off my nose to spite my face. Or to put it another way, I may be a 'simple' country lass, but I don't have straw growing out my arse – or whatever it is you humans say.

* * * * *

THIRTEEN

AS I SAY, it's funny how you can remember things that happened years and years in the past, yet still forget what you've done or even where you were a few minutes ago. All part of getting old, according to the Boss and Lady B. Something else that's just nature's way, I suppose, and something else that isn't for me to even try and understand. When I say 'something else', I'm harking back to the sorry outcome of my 'dalliance' with that creep Shuggie, which was the first of these temporary memory-loss events that actually bothered me. Most examples after that have been when one of my humans has suddenly appeared in front of me and asked what I was doing there, which was usually somewhere perfectly normal, like in the garden or here in the yard.

'You're getting a bit wandered,' the Boss would tell me with a chuckle, before patting me on the head and adding, 'Aye, a wee bit muddled.'

I didn't know what he was talking about, because words like 'wandered' and 'muddled' meant nothing to me, impressive though my grasp of the human vocabulary had become. All I knew was that I'd sort of wake up, standing in a place I knew like the back of my paw, and not have a clue why I was there. And the most weird thing about it was that I realised right away that I hadn't been asleep, so couldn't *actually* have been waking up.

'Losing it,' was how Lady B put it on one occasion. She said it under her breath, probably hoping I wouldn't hear. But I did, and felt a bit miffed, even though I didn't really understand why. Anyway, no harm was being done, so I didn't give it much thought. Well, none at all, actually, until that one particular time I said I'd tell you about … *if* I remembered.

*

IT HAPPENED QUITE recently – maybe about a month ago – and I woke up in the hill field, sitting on that same knowe I'd sat on with the Boss soon after I came here. That was the time he told me about all the places you could see from up there; the same day he pulled a prank on me with the so-called stampeding cattle coming to a sudden stop just before they trampled all over us. In any event, I woke up and thought I'd been dreaming about being in that very spot. Then I realised I hadn't been dreaming at all, so couldn't have been sleeping *or*, for that matter, waking up. I don't mind confessing that I came over all cold and shivery. I was scared, because I couldn't understand what was happening. OK, I know I'd had similar experiences before, like the one I just mentioned involving that sleekit fleabag Shuggie, and those few minor ones when the Boss or Lady B had found me in what they called a 'wandered' or 'losing-it' state near the house. But this was different somehow. The weird thing was that I didn't know where I was. I didn't recognise the place, other than having just seen it in what had *seemed* like a dream. To make matters worse, I hadn't a clue where I'd come from. I was lost – simple as that – and I could feel panic rising at the very thought. This was a feeling I had never experienced before: all alone in a strange place, with no way of finding my way home – *if* I even had a home to go to.

Then something even more weird happened. I saw a man walking directly towards me over the crest of the hill. There was nothing even vaguely familiar about him, so when he got closer I started to growl, warning him off. It was spooky the way I could see his eyes, yet wasn't getting any vibes from him at all. I felt threatened, but instead of doing what comes naturally, which would have been to go for his ankles, I lay down in front of him, whimpering. I was ashamed of myself – I really was – but was too confused *and* scared to do anything about it.

'So, found you at last, Jen,' the man said. 'But what's wrong – don't you recognise me?'

I stayed pressed to the ground, trembling and more confused than ever now.

'Come on, you daft old besom,' he chuckled, 'sit up and give me a smile – no need to *coorie doon* like that.'

'Coorie doon ... coorie doon ... coorie doon.' The words meant nothing, yet there was something

vaguely familiar about them too.

The man continued to speak, but all I heard was the echo of those two words going round and round in my head. Then, after a while, he popped his fingers and I glanced up to see that he was leaning forward, patting his chest and smiling.

'What? No flying back flip for me today?'

It was as if a fog suddenly started to lift from my mind. I remembered the man's voice speaking those very words a long, long time ago. I stared into his eyes and could see now that they had a kindly look to them, a look which, like his voice, I was beginning to realise I knew from somewhere. I started to feel less afraid, and made no attempt to shy away when he knelt down beside me and gently stroked my head.

'Come on, lass,' he said, 'time to go home now, hmm?' He reached into his pocket and brought out a piece of baler twine, which he looped carefully through my collar. 'Do you remember the only other time I used this as a lead?' He gave another little chuckle. 'Yes, that's right – just after you'd had that *courting* session with old Shuggie and I wanted to make sure you wouldn't head off with him for a repeat performance. How could you forget, eh?'

Well, actually, I *had* forgotten at that particular moment, but as we walked home the memory of that unfortunate experience – along with a few more enjoyable ones – gradually began to return. But it was only when we reached the farmyard and I listened to the Boss telling his side of the story to Lady B that I realised just how puzzling my presence in the hill field had been.

According to the Boss, I had gone on what he called 'walkabout' across the wee paddock in front of the house earlier in the day. As it happens, there was nothing out of the ordinary about that, except I didn't return after my usual hour or so 'sniffing about the hedgerows'. Several hours passed with still no sign of me, so the Boss, suspecting that something was amiss, decided to mount a search. To cut a long story short, he eventually came across me at the farthest point on the farm, but why I had gone there to sit doing nothing was a mystery.

Lady B crouched down and cupped my face in her hands, the way she always does when she's feeling sorry for me. 'Oh, you poor wee thing,' she crooned. 'Getting a wee bit wandered right enough, hmm? Well, old age doesn't come by itself, they say. But never you mind, pet, we'll take good care of you, never fear.'

I was still trying to come to terms with having remembered nothing about anything or anyone in my life for so much of that day, which frightened me. The Boss and Lady B began to discuss the matter in lowered voices. I listened carefully, but most of the words I did manage to pick up were new to me. They mentioned something that sounded like 'Demensher', which they said they'd speak to the vet about, so I took it to be a germ of some kind. I'd had one of those germ things before – painful – in my ear – and the vet killed it with drops. But how could he kill this 'Demensher' germ? I mean, it wasn't actually hurting me anywhere, so where would he put the drops? Then I heard Lady B whispering to the Boss about me going somewhere called 'Senile', which she said you get to by going 'away with the fairies'. Something like that anyway. I immediately tried sending thought waves telling her she was wrong: I was perfectly happy here, thanks very much, and had no wish to go anywhere else. But I'm not sure she got the message.

Anyhow, the Boss put my mind at ease a bit by patting my head and assuring me they'd keep an eye on me from now on. In fact, it'd be best if I just hung about the yard most of the time and didn't go anywhere on my own, just in case I took another one of those wee 'turns'. He'd make sure I didn't get bored, though – promising to take me with him whenever possible. And I don't mind telling you I felt *very* relieved about that. Senile? No, I didn't fancy the sound of that place at all.

THINGS WENT ALONG without any noticeable recurrence of the memory loss problem for a while after that. Well, in saying this, what I really mean is any recurrence that was likely to be noticed by anybody but me. You see, there *were* a few occasions when I went to do something or other, but on getting there had completely forgotten what it was I'd intended to do. That was *all* I'd forgotten, though. I mean, I remembered going there, being there, and going away again, so it was only the *purpose* of the visit that had slipped my mind, that's all. For that reason, I wasn't particularly worried about these wee 'turns', as they obviously hadn't prevented me from doing anything important – otherwise I wouldn't have forgotten what it was I intended doing in the first place, if you see what I mean. And anyway, on most occasions I *did* remember what I'd forgotten after a while, and it usually turned out to be nothing of any significance after all. Just one of those things that happen as you get older, I told myself – like the stiffness in my joints.

Talking about that, although I hate to admit it, there have been times lately when the Boss has even had to help me up after I've been lying down for a while. And that really is embarrassing, especially for an independent-natured Border collie like me. But the Boss doesn't make a big thing about it; doesn't even say a word, just whistles a wee tune or something then carries on with whatever he's busy with. He's very good that way, the Boss – doesn't make your embarrassment even worse by mentioning your stiff joints when he's helping you up. I'll give him that, and I appreciate it. I really do.

Also, I wouldn't blame him for the bit of bother I found myself in a week or so back. After all, he could hardly be expected to keep an eye on me for *every* minute of the day, although I know he really did try his best. And as you'd expect, so did Lady B whenever she was looking after things for him. Even so, I *did* manage to slip away unnoticed this particular day, and I can't tell you how or why, only that it turned out to be another blackout, like the Shuggie episode and that later one up the hill field.

The first I knew about it was when I sort of came to in the yard and this stranger was sounding off at the Boss about his dog wandering around on the roadside and making cars swerve all over the place.

An uncontrolled dog like that was a danger to the public, he said, and should be tied up. And what's more, it wasn't the first time he'd seen the stupid animal lurking about out there. 'Mark my words,' he snapped, 'if it happens again, I'll be reporting you and your bloody dog to the police!'

I could see the Boss was itching to have a go back at him, but thought better of it. After all, if what the man had said was true – and there was no reason to doubt it – he was entitled to be annoyed.

'He had your best interests at heart,' the Boss told to me after the man had stormed off, 'even if he had a damned strange way of showing it. But anyway, we'll have to think about what we can do to make sure it doesn't happen again, eh?' He gave me a wink and ruffled the top of my head. 'Don't worry, lass, we'll sort it out … somehow.'

Although I'd understood the gist of what had been said, I was still in a bewildered state, with absolutely no recollection of what this stranger had been complaining about. It was the same helpless feeling that had gripped me after the episode in the hill field: knowing something bad was happening to me, but unable to understand what it was or how to stop it. It struck home then that, no matter how much it rankled, none of the collie attributes I was so proud of would help me now. Only my human friends could do that.

Yet, as much as I trusted the Boss to do what was right, I wasn't at all happy about what he suggested. He'd never have contemplated it before, he told Lady B when she came out to see what all the commotion had been about, but the only sure way of preventing me from doing anything as dangerous as that again would be to do as the man said. There was nothing else for it, he shrugged, they'd have to keep me tied up.

Lady B looked as shocked as I felt. 'But that'd be cruel,' she gasped. 'She's never been tied up before. It would break her heart.'

The Boss assured her that he understood all that, but stressed it wasn't as if I'd be tied up *all* the time – only when I was going to be left on my own. 'Cruel it may be,' he agreed, 'but it's a helluva lot kinder than risking her being killed on the road.'

I STOOD BY Lady B's side as the Boss set about attaching a length of fence wire to the foot of the door post of my wee house, which sat in the corner between the old byre and the barn. He then ran the wire parallel to the ground along to the opposite end of the byre, where he fixed it securely to an old tethering ring. Next he looped a piece of clothes line round the wire, beckoned me across, bent down and tied the loose end to my collar.

'There you are, Jen,' he said, standing back up. 'Plenty of scope for you to run back and forth, or slip into your house when you feel like it, or even have a wee snooze in your favourite spot against the wall there.' He glanced down at me, but avoided making eye contact. 'Just look at this,' he breezed, moving the looped end of the rope to and fro along the wire. 'It's not like being tied up at all, is it?'

Who was he trying to kid? For the first time in my life I felt that the freedom I valued so much was about to come to an end, and in the most undignified way as well. Me, a Border collie, and from one of the best bloodlines this side of Australia, tethered to the side of a byre as if I was a common junk yard dog like the ones you see on the telly when humans are going about shooting each other. And I was expected to feel fine about it? No way! OK, I could tell the Boss was making a big effort to appear upbeat, but he was failing miserably, and the expression on his face showed that he knew it. I got that, and I felt for him, but what I still didn't understand was why I was having these bouts of memory loss and why the Boss couldn't fix the problem. He was a human after all, and therefore equipped with all the necessary skills. I mean, like I've said, I'd seen him and the vets taking the nuts off bull calves and snipping the extra tits off baby heifers, never mind burning their newly sprouted horns off as well. So where was the problem in killing off this 'Demensher' germ, or whatever it was called, even if it wasn't as straightforward as squirting drops in my ear? Everything was possible for humans … wasn't it?

Lady B bent down beside me and took the rope in her hand. 'I can see you're upset, pet,' she murmured, 'but you'll get used to it, and we'll make sure you aren't tied to this except when it's *absolutely* necessary. I promise.' She turned to the Boss. 'Just look at the poor wee thing – totally miserable. When did you ever see Jen standing with her tail between her legs like that before? She *is* a free spirit, and this'll be like a prison sentence for her.'

The Boss didn't answer, but I could tell he agreed.

Yet he seemed unable to do anything about it, and that scared me. I wandered over to my wee house and lay down outside, trying to ignore the rope while willing myself to think of more pleasant things. But it was difficult – *really* difficult.

Lady B then said something to the Boss under her breath. It was one of those times when she thought I wouldn't hear, forgetting just how super-sensitive my ears are. I wasn't in the mood to pay all that much attention anyway, but what I did pick up was that the length of clothes line he'd used to tether me was bound to meet with the same fate as the *Swing Ball* string: I'd just gnaw through it, no matter how long it took. She was right about that, but if she'd had as much sense as I used to give her credit for, she'd have kept it to herself.

As it was, the Boss had been of the same opinion. 'Maybe I'll come with you when you go to the shops today. I could pop into the plumber's and buy a yard or two of that chain you yank for flushing old toilets.'

'*Chain*'. I knew that word. It's what the Boss used for hauling rocks off the fields – big, heavy boulders that had been nudged up by the plough. Even in the days when my teeth were sound, I'd never have been able to chew my way through that stuff. No, I didn't like the sound of this at *all*.

I closed my eyes and pretended to be having a nap while they went through the motions of tidying up the yard. It was obvious they were only waiting to see how I'd take to having my movements curtailed when I woke up, but I wasn't about to oblige. It was humiliating enough to be tethered like this without giving a public demonstration of how the mighty had fallen – if that's the right expression.

Anyhow, I must have dozed off after all, and eventually stirred to the sound of the car leaving the yard, with the Boss and Lady B bound, I assumed, for the shops ... and that dreaded piece of chain. I had never felt so downhearted in all my life, and it really takes an awful lot to dampen the spirits of a Border collie, believe me. Under normal circumstances, I'd probably have gone no more than a few paces to my usual spot against the byre wall, to relax until my humans returned, or an unsuspecting sales rep happened by to keep me amused. But the very idea of being restrained like this sent a feeling of panic coursing through me. My eyes darted around the yard, and although I'd been familiar with every nook and cranny for all those years, it felt as if I was in a strange, alien place, full of threatening shapes and shadows.

All I wanted to do was escape. Now.

I found myself running away, only to be jerked to a shuddering stop, reeling head-over-heels and gasping for breath. My heart was racing as I started to pull frantically at the rope – tugging, biting, worrying it until my teeth hurt. I tried to make off again, but with the same painful result. I could hear myself barking and yelping, yet seemed detached from what was happening as well. I wasn't sure where I was, why I was there, or where I had come from, but could see the clasp of my collar lying at my feet. It had been wrenched off, with the rope still firmly attached.

Then the all-too-familiar curtain of oblivion began to close round me once more.

* * * * *

– *FOURTEEN* –

THE NEXT THING I remember was coming to in the middle of the road outside the farm gate. I was lying there as relaxed and contented as when basking in my favourite spot against the byre wall. But instead of the sleepy chirping of sparrows that would greet me when waking up in the yard, all I could hear now was the violent screech of car tyres. It immediately dredged up memories of that morning many years earlier when little Boy Two was so tragically taken from us on this same stretch of road, and I felt a chill running down my spine. Then, as the mist began to clear from my mind, my ears were bombarded by the blasting of car horns, angry shouting and the crunch of metal colliding with metal. Confusion reigned all around me, and although I realised where I was, I had no recollection of how I came to be there. I attempted to get up, but the stiffness in my legs made it a slow and painful process.

'Get that bloody animal off the road!' a voice called out. 'And be quick about it, before somebody gets killed here!'

I felt a hand grabbing me by the collar, and I instinctively tried to twist round and fight back. The response was a growl of, 'Don't you try and bite *me*, ye wee bugger!' followed by a dig in the ribs, which was delivered with enough force to knock the wind out of me.

I must have blacked out again, for I've no idea what happened next. But when I came round this time, I was lying on the grass verge with the Boss crouching over me. He was shaking me gently. 'It's OK, Jen – everything's gonna be fine. Come on now – wake up – there's a good girl.'

Everything was hazy, but I could make out a man in dark clothes standing beside the Boss. After a few moments I recognised him as a policeman I'd recently seen talking to the Boss on the opposite side of the yard from where I was sitting. If you were to ask me *exact*ly when that was, I'd probably say the previous day. But my memory of recent events is getting really wobbly – all over the place – so I can't be absolutely sure. Anyway, I hadn't heard what they were talking about, but I'd caught them looking in my direction a few times, and they both had pretty serious expressions on their faces. I noticed they were wearing similar expressions now.

'I can't understand it, Sergeant,' said the Boss. 'We left her securely tied up, I promise you. And we were only away half an hour at the most. So, somehow, she must have –'

'Wrenched the ring off her collar,' the policeman butted in. He nodded down at me. 'See for yourself, sir. It's missing. Aye, I've seen it happen with tethered dogs often enough before, especially collies. Nah, nothing'll stop them if they take it into their heads to break free. They just sort of flip. I've seen it happen.'

The Boss looked at me with a sad smile, then shook his head. 'Trust you, Jen. Queen of the free spirits, right enough, eh?'

The policeman explained that one of the neighbouring farm lads had carried me off the road. 'Said he had to give her a wee thump in the ribs to calm her down. He apologised for that, but reckoned she was gonna bite him, and there was another car coming round the corner.' I had been lucky twice, he added, gesturing towards two badly dented cars parked on the verge nearby, but if the drivers of those vehicles hadn't swerved to miss me, it might well have been third time *un*lucky.

'Yeah,' the Boss nodded, 'I'll have to thank the lad for risking being savaged. Not that Jen would have gone through with it,' he swiftly stressed. 'She's never been known to bite *any*body.'

'Maybe not,' the Sergeant replied, 'but it's different when they've been tied up – especially collies. As I say, I've seen how they react.' He cast me an a sideways glance. 'Bonkers.'

In the wake of so much confusion, it was comforting to hear the policeman referring to me by my old nickname, and it made me think he maybe had a soft spot for me, even if I *had* been the cause of the two cars bumping into each other.

He pointed them out to the Boss. 'You'd better go and exchange details with the owners there. They'll likely be claiming on your insurance, so I hope you're covered.'

The Boss winced. 'Yeah, you and me both.'

'That's your problem,' shrugged the policeman, 'but you can take some consolation from the fact that the outcome of this incident could have been a lot worse. You could have been standing here accused of causing serious injury to, or the death of, an innocent person or persons by failing to keep a dog under proper control. It's the law.' He looked the Boss in the eye and stated bluntly, 'And you can't say you weren't warned following previous complaints.'

'Yes, I know, I know,' the Boss muttered, lowering his eyes and looking suitably remorseful. 'It won't happen again.'

'Well, I told you before what the position would be if it *did* happen again – and it has.' The policeman paused, then added in hushed tones, 'You know what you have to do, sir. And if you fail to comply, the matter will be taken out of your hands.'

I wondered what he'd meant by that. Could it be that he'd told the Boss how to get rid of the 'Demensher' germ that was playing havoc with my behaviour? Well, no matter what he'd meant, it sounded as if the Boss would be in some kind of trouble if he didn't do it. But to tell the truth, I was even more confused than ever now.

* * *

KNOWING WHAT YOU know now about my past record as a live-in house dog, you may be surprised to learn that I slept in the farmhouse last night. But I did, and it surprised me too. That said, I hadn't been *too* surprised when I saw Lady B waiting in the yard for the Boss and me after the incident out there on the road. The Boss was leading me on his trusty piece of baler twine, by the way – probably worried that I might head off on my own again. He needn't have concerned himself, though, for I'd be lying if I said this latest bout of memory loss hadn't taught me a lesson. Discovering that I might have been run over *and* had endangered the lives of some humans made it sink in that there was something very bad happening to me. In all my life I'd never have behaved like that intentionally. I really wouldn't.

Lady B knew this too, and I think that's why she gave me a big cuddle when I came back into the yard. She didn't say anything, but I noticed there were tears in her eyes, which was all the proof I needed that she was just as worried about my well-being as I was myself. So was the Boss. I'd seen that as plain as you like when he was being lectured by that policeman. That's the thing about the Boss – you can tell he's worried about something when he lowers his eyes and looks down in the dumps like that. He's usually pretty good at setting things right, though, so I just hoped he would be up to sorting things out this time. Like I say, I knew there was something bad happening to me, and I didn't know how to fix it by myself, which frightened me. It honestly did.

I don't know how many years it's been since I last spent a night in the house. Most of my life, I suppose, although it seemed like only yesterday. Of course, I was still well used to what it *looks* like, due to the fact that I've been making those 'secret' afternoon visits to the Boss right up to a few days ago. But one thing that did differ from the last time I'd been in there at night was that I wasn't 'encouraged' to move back from the fireside. Also, the boys weren't at home and the Boss and Lady B seemed content to just sit on the couch in silence, except on a couple of occasions when they talked about me. They probably thought I hadn't noticed, as I was lying in front of them with my eyes closed, enjoying the peaceful atmosphere that had replaced the usual jabber of the Boss arguing with the telly. But as I've told you before, the thing about us dogs is that our ears are always switched on, even when you think we're sleeping.

And what I heard the Boss and Lady B discussing – very quietly, incidentally – made interesting listening, even if it wasn't all that encouraging. But I'm not saying they were criticising me in any way, if that's what you're thinking. In actual fact, and surprising as it may seem, Lady B didn't even mention the effect my proximity to the fire had on my contribution to the air quality in the room. No, what they were discussing, as far as I could make out, was how this 'Demensher' germ could attack humans as well. For example, they'd heard about one old lady who sometimes went 'walkabout' too, and didn't recognise her family when they eventually found her. They talked about a few other human 'cases', but I gave up trying to catch what they were saying after a while. It was all a bit depressing, hearing about so many humans who couldn't be fixed. What I had been hoping to hear was something about how *humans* could get rid of the 'Demensher' germ in a *dog*, bearing in mind I'd overheard the policeman telling the Boss that he knew what had to be done next. But no such news was forthcoming, so I just contented myself with enjoying this unexpected treat, until the warmth of the fire became too much for comfort. That's when I padded off to the coolness of my old bed, the knobbly rubber door mat inside the back door. And I couldn't have been happier.

*

WHICH TAKES US to where we are today, with me lying here beside the vet's car, thinking back over my life and recounting a few of the most interesting bits for you.

Jim the vet arrived first thing this morning, just as the Boss and I were coming out of the house. As was his usual way, Jim spoke to me first. 'Morning, Jen,' he winked. 'Been behaving yourself, have you?'

If he was alluding to the much-regretted 'mistake' I'd made with the reprobate Shuggie, it would have been an attempt at humour distinctly lacking in taste, and I'd have been entitled to feel affronted. But I liked Jim, so I gave him the benefit of the doubt and beamed across a welcoming vibe, which I hoped he had the ability to understand. What I'm getting at is that you'd reckon vets, of all humans, would be able to exchange thought waves with dogs as competently as the best, but when you take into account all the different kinds of animals they have to deal with, it's maybe asking a bit too much. I mean, who's to say, for instance, that a horse beaming across a message that it has a pain in the arse is just as easy for a vet to understand as a cat vibing him that she's up the duff? It's an intriguing proposition, and one I'll probably get round to considering in more depth sometime … if I remember.

'Well, we've a lot to do,' Jim said to the Boss while pulling on his overalls. 'Do you want to start with…?' He nodded in my direction.

'No, no, she'll be fine for now,' the boss came back, sounding a touch too nonchalant, I thought. 'Just, you know, just maybe give her something for her … ehm … for her joints. Yeah, I notice she's a wee bit stiff this morning, so… '

Jim gave him a knowing look, but didn't say a word. He rummaged about in the boot of his car, then knelt down beside me, opened my mouth with one hand, and popped something down my throat with the other. 'A wee sweetie for you, Jen. That should help things along.'

They're really good at popping something down your throat, vets. I'll give them that. This was my first experience of the process, I admit, but I'd seen them doing it often enough with cattle – stuffing tablets as big as a golf ball down their throats sometimes. And they never seem to get bitten. I mean, you wouldn't want to be chomped by a cow's back teeth, believe me. Just think of the power they need to crunch up chunks of raw Swedes and you'll know what I'm talking about. Same with dogs, of course, because you wouldn't want to get a piece of your hand clamped between a dog's back teeth either. But these vets, well, they really have the knack of popping pills down your throat before you can have a go at their fingers. Really clever, when you think about it.

'Just a wee tranquillizer,' Jim told the Boss. 'Should keep her nice and comfy.'

Well, I don't know what was in that sweetie, but I can tell you it certainly made me feel good. No kidding, I'd never felt so relaxed in my life, and there was certainly no risk of me going off on another one of those 'walkabouts', if that's what you're thinking. Oh yes, a clever thing, that sweetie of the vet's. When it first kicked in, I felt what you humans would probably call a 'buzz'. I sort of felt how the Boss looks when he's been drinking that sheep's piss stuff – if that makes any sense. But after a while I just felt kind of mellow, and that felt even better, to be honest.

Mark you, when I said there was no danger of me wandering off again, I noticed Lady B had been keeping a watchful eye on me through the kitchen window – just in case, no doubt. I must say I hadn't been paying *particular* attention, but every time I happened to glance towards the house, there she was looking through the window, while washing the dishes or cleaning vegetables or scrubbing car mats or whatever. She didn't look too happy, though. Sort of weepy, actually, which is maybe quite understandable under the circumstances. I mean to say, who would want to be standing at the kitchen sink slaving away at stuff like that? Not me anyway. And in case you're wondering, I'm not forgetting I said I'd take Lady B on as my housekeeper, *if* our situations were reversed. But I'd also make a point of ensuring she was happier in her work than she looked today. Fair's fair, after all.

However, maybe I'm just thinking too much, for if I have a fault at all it's that I do tend to think too much at times. You know what I mean: all that stuff about how we dogs would run things if we had fingers – and thumbs too, of course. But it's never going to happen, is it? So why waste time thinking about it? No, now that I've had a chance to go over some of the things that have happened in my life, I can honestly say I wouldn't have changed any of it … except maybe losing that wee pup of mine, but I'd rather not dwell on that, if you don't mind. The good times have far outweighed the bad, as the saying goes, and I'm really grateful, for not all dogs have been as lucky as I have, and I realise that, I really do. Then again, not all humans have enjoyed having the company of a dog as faithful, fun-loving, easy-going and, if I may say so, intelligent as me – even if I do tend to think a bit too much at times.

I'm just sorry this 'Demensher' germ has made me act in ways that have caused concern and trouble for the Boss and Lady B of late. And now that I think about it, that *is* one thing I would have changed, given the choice. But I know they already understand that, and this is why they've brought the vet here to do whatever it takes to cure me of the ailment once and for all. And on second thoughts, I have to say it was actually very considerate of the Boss to get on with other things first. I mean, he must have picked up a vibe – albeit a subconscious one – that this would be a good time for me to take the weight off my joints, take it easy for a while and reflect on my life. I've enjoyed doing it too, thanks in no small measure, I suspect, to the relaxing effect of Jim's 'wee sweetie'.

The Boss and the vet were away quite a while, castrating calves or testing heifers for brucellosis or whatever else, and although the time passed quickly enough for me, I was glad to see them coming back into the yard at last, and all set, I hoped, to do what was needed to help me be my old self again. They were both looking a bit down in the mouth, I must say, but I suppose spending so much time separating bull calves from their testicles would tend to make any human glum. Any *male* human anyway.

Back in the day, I'd have bounded over to meet them and would have treated the Boss to a good old flying back flip. That would have cheered him up all right. But to repeat a saying I've used already today, the mind was willing, but the body refused to cooperate – or words to that effect. As a result, I had to leave the Boss to find his own way up from whatever dumps he'd found himself down in.

Still, Jim the vet did manage a smile when he got to the car, and although it didn't quite reach his eyes, at least he tried, and he even patted my head, which was a first. 'Sorry to keep you waiting, old girl,' he said. 'Not long now, though.' He went to fetch something from the back of his car again, but I couldn't see what it was. I don't mind confessing, though, that if it had been another of his 'wee sweeties', I wouldn't have complained. But it wasn't, as he explained to the Boss...

'It'll only be a wee pinprick. She'll hardly feel a thing, and after a few seconds ... well ...' He paused and offered me another little smile, then lowered his voice to a whisper. 'Then everything will be fine again, eh, Jen? Yes, of course it will.'

Still speaking softly, he asked the Boss to kneel down beside me, then pick me up and cradle me like a baby with my head resting in the crook of his arm. It was exactly as if I'd landed there after my usual welcoming 'trick', except that I hadn't been able to perform it unaided this time, and that was another first. But I wasn't bothered about that. After all, Jim had just hinted that I'd be back to my old self again soon, and I was quite content to be lying there while he got on with working his magic.

It was then that I looked up at the Boss's face, and now that it was close to mine I could see the look in his eyes quite clearly. But it wasn't the glum look I'd been expecting. In fact, it wasn't one I'd seen before, although it did remind me of the way Lady B had looked while watching me through the kitchen window earlier. There was something there, something profoundly sad, and the tears welling in the Boss's eyes helped foster a thought I'd been trying hard to suppress since seeing him return to the yard.

I heard the vet say again that it would be just a pinprick, and the Boss pulled me close to his chest and stroked my head.

'It'll soon be over now, Jen,' he murmured, his voice breaking. 'Everything's fine – everything's fine – don't you worry.' His hand passed over my eyes, closing them gently. 'That's it, lass ... sleep now ... sleep now ... sleep now ... '

I found myself growing drowsier and drowsier, then, as if in a dream, I was floating high above the yard, bathed in a bright light and looking down on where I'd been lying in the Boss's arms only a moment before. The vet's car had gone, yet I was still there, scampering about as friskily as ever, having fun like old times, catching stones and playing games in the company of my little family. And I was as happy as I'd ever been in my life.

Then the light that had been surrounding me began to fade, and as the image below me grew ever fainter, I heard the Boss's voice calling out to me:

'*RUN FREE NOW, JEN ... RUN AND PLAY ... RUN AND PLAY TO YOUR HEART'S CONTENT, LASS ... THAT'S A GOOD GIRL.*'

* * *

THE END

If you enjoyed this book, you may also like the following set-in Scotland titles by Peter Kerr:

'THISTLE SOUP'

- An Autobiographical Prequel to Snowball Oranges -

East Lothian is 'The Garden of Scotland' and the setting for this delightfully idiosyncratic story of country life, from the time of the Second World War onwards. Often hilarious, always heartfelt and at times sad, this book will appeal, not only to those who are interested in the Scotland of today, but also to people who recall, or have been told about, rural ways that are gone for ever.

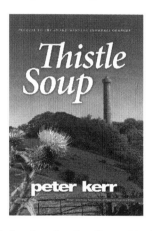

"The story of his boyhood, a family and its farms. Amusing, interesting, moving and true to-life." (The Scotsman)

"Beautifully written, gently humorous – a real gem of a book." (Amazon UK)

(Paperback ISBN 978-0-9573062-2-6)

(Kindle E-book ISBN 978-0-9574963-0-9)

www.peter-kerr.co.uk

'DON'T CALL ME CLYDE!'

- Jazz Journey of a Sixties Stomper -

(An Autobiographical 'Companion' to Thistle Soup)

The Clyde Valley Stompers became, in the 1950s, Scotland's premier jazz band and first-ever super group. In 1961, at just twenty years of age, Peter 'Pete' Kerr inherited leadership of 'The Clydes' after they'd move their base from Glasgow to London. Despite many set-backs, the band stormed the charts the following year with their version of Peter and the Wolf, and were launched into the glitzy world of mainstream popular music. But, as Peter would discover to his cost, it was also a world tainted by greed. This is a story that will surprise and amuse in equal measure – and will occasionally shock too!

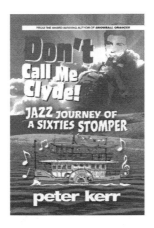

"Laced with all the wit and eye for the telling detail one expects from this best-selling author. As intensely readable as it is enjoyable." (London Jazz News)

"Entertaining and intriguing, even if you're not into jazz." (Toun Cryer Magazine)

"The story of a young man realising his dream of playing jazz for a living." (The Glasgow Herald)

(Paperback ISBN 978-0-9576586-2-2)

(Kindle E-book ISBN 978-0-9576586-3-9)

'FIDDLER ON THE MAKE'
- *The Cuddyford Chronicles* -

When the sleepy village of Cuddyford is colonised by
well-heeled retirees and big-city commuters, Jigger McCloud,
a jack-the-lad local farmer with a talent for playing the
fiddle and an eye for the ladies, isn't slow to make
a quick buck at their expense. Comic shenanigans,
quirky characters and sinister ploys abound in this
not-everyday story of country folk.

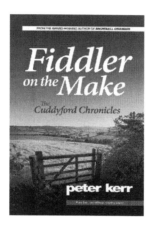

"A hoot – pure fun – an observation on the absurd."
(Welsh Books Council)

"A delicious, delightful and devilishly funny gem of a novel."
(Stornoway Gazette)

(Paperback ISBN 978-0-9576586-1-5)

(Kindle E-book ISBN 978-0-9574963-9-2)

www.peter-kerr.co.uk

'THE SPORRAN CONNECTION'

- Bob Burns Investigates -

The second in a trilogy of tongue-in-cheek Bob Burns
mysteries finds the droll Scots sleuth aided once again by
the stunning, game-for-anything forensic scientist Julie
Bryson and keener-than-bright rookie cop Andy Green.
The action shifts from southern Scotland to Sicily, New
York and a remote Hebridean island as the line between
the good and bad guys becomes increasingly blurred.

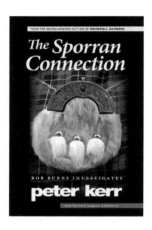

*"A really gripping page-turner that's peppered
with laughs." (Amazon UK)*

*"Well off the wall ... escapist and liberally laced
with humour." (Edinburgh Evening News)*

(Paperback ISBN 978-0-9573062-5-7)

(Kindle E-book ISBN 978-0-9574963-4-7)

www.peter-kerr.co.uk

'THE *OTHER* MONARCH OF THE GLEN'

- A Quirky Caledonian Caper -

An opportunity to acquire a fortune arises when the flat-broke and feckless laird of Strathsporran Castle uncovers a valuable work of art – but only if its existence remains secret. Skulduggery and amorous anomalies abound as the laird becomes embroiled in an audacious scam with two unlikely shooting guests. But who's conning who? And what other secrets will the grouse moors of Strathsporran reveal? Pure fun – a pacey, racy Highland fling.

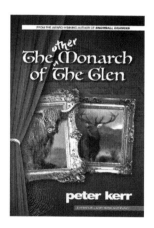

"An entertaining, laugh-out-loud tale ... a high-spirited and crazy caper" (Majorca Daily Bulletin)

"A pleasantly bonkers yarn of the sort Tom Sharpe used to spin." (London Jazz News)

(Paperback ISBN 9780-0-9576586-8-4)

(Kindle E-book ASIN B0781QRXMV)

www.peter-kerr.co.uk

'GOBLIN HALL'
- A Fantasy Adventure -

A humour-spiced family fantasy named after a haunted
chamber that lies beneath the ruins of Yester Castle near
Gifford in East Lothian. Two young children are lured into
the subterranean world of Zorn, an evil sorcerer who is using
them as bait to ensnare his arch enemy Mungo, a lovable
but dippy old wizard friend of the children. Goblins
and monsters abound as the kids journey through the
underworld to a good-versus-evil showdown in Zorn's lair.
But ... not everything may be as it seems!

*"Both children and adults will be captivated by this
exciting story." (East Lothian Life Magazine)*

*"A magical fantasy adventure for all the family."
(Edinburgh Life Magazine)*

(Paperback ISBN 978-0-9576586-9-1)

(Kindle E-Book ASIN B0871LGJCV)

www.peter-kerr.co.uk

ALSO BY PETER KERR:

'SNOWBALL ORANGES'
- *One Mallorcan Winter* -

First in the bestselling series of five books charting the Kerr
family's often hilarious adventures after leaving Scotland to
grow oranges for a living on the Spanish island of Mallorca.

"Immensely engaging and amusing."

"Full of life and colour – a haven of Mediterranean sunshine."

*"The story is carried effortless through on an entertaining
raft of humour"*

(Paperback ISBN 978-1-78685-042-3)

(Kindle E-book ASIN B06XKMQVLZ)

Full details of this and all Peter's other titles
are on his website: **www.peter-kerr.co.uk**

Printed in Great Britain
by Amazon

72234724R00123